THE HOUSEBREAKER OF SHADY HILL

and Other Stories

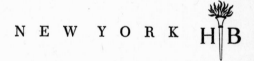

NEW YORK

John Cheever THE
HOUSEBREAKER
OF SHADY HILL
and Other Stories

HARPER & BROTHERS

PUBLISHERS

All but one of these stories first appeared in *The New Yorker*. The author is grateful to that magazine for permission to reprint them.

Library of Congress catalog card number: 58-11397

for VIRGINIA AND DUDLEY SCHOALES

CONTENTS

THE HOUSEBREAKER OF SHADY HILL

✱ **MY NAME** is Johnny Hake. I'm thirty-six years old, stand five feet eleven in my socks, weigh one hundred and forty-two pounds stripped, and am, so to speak, naked at the moment and talking into the dark. I was conceived in the Hotel St. Regis, born in the Presbyterian Hospital, raised on Sutton Place, christened and confirmed in St. Bartholomew's, and I drilled with the Knickerbocker Greys, played football and baseball in Central Park, learned to chin myself on the framework of East Side apartment-house canopies, and met my wife (Christina Lewis) at one of those big cotillions at the Waldorf. I served four years in the Navy, have four kids now, and live in a *banlieue* called Shady Hill. We have a nice house with a garden and a place outside for cooking meat, and on summer nights, sitting there with the kids and looking into the front of Christina's dress as she bends over to salt the steaks, or just gazing at the lights in Heaven, I am as thrilled as I am thrilled by more hardy and dangerous pursuits, and I guess this is what is meant by the pain and sweetness of life.

I went to work right after the war for a parablendeum manufacturer, and seemed on the way to making this my life.

3

The firm was patriarchal; that is, the old man would start you on one thing and then switch you to another, and he had his finger in every pie—the Jersey mill and the processing plant in Nashville—and behaved as if he had wool-gathered the whole firm during a cat nap. I stayed out of the old man's way as nimbly as I could, and behaved in his presence as if he had shaped me out of clay with his own hands and breathed the fire of life into me. He was the kind of despot who needed a front, and this was Gil Bucknam's job. He was the old man's right hand, front, and peacemaker, and he could garnish any deal with the humanity the old man lacked, but he started staying out of the office—at first for a day or two, then for two weeks, and then for longer. When he returned, he would complain about stomach trouble or eyestrain, although anyone could see that he was looped. This was not so strange, since hard drinking was one of the things he had to do for the firm. The old man stood it for a year and then came into my office one morning and told me to get up to Bucknam's apartment and give him the sack.

This was as devious and dirty as sending an office boy to can the chairman of the board. Bucknam was my superior and my senior by many years, a man who condescended to do so whenever he bought me a drink, but this was the way the old man operated, and I knew what I had to do. I called the Bucknam apartment, and Mrs. Bucknam said that I could see Gil that afternoon. I had lunch alone and hung around the office until about three, when I *walked* from our midtown office to the Bucknams' apartment, in the East Seventies. It was early in the fall—the World Series was being played—and a thunderstorm was entering the city. I could hear the

4

noise of big guns and smell the rain when I got to the Buck-nams' place. Mrs. Bucknam let me in, and all the troubles of that past year seemed to be in her face, hastily concealed by a thick coat of powder. I've never seen such burned-out eyes, and she was wearing one of those old-fashioned garden-party dresses with big flowers on it. (They had three kids in college, I knew, and a schooner with a hired hand, and many other expenses.) Gil was in bed, and Mrs. Bucknam let me into the bedroom. The storm was about to break now, and everything stood in a gentle half darkness so much like dawn that it seemed as if we should be sleeping and dreaming, and not bringing one another bad news.

Gil was jolly and lovable and condescending, and said that he was *so* glad to see me; he had bought a lot of presents for my children when he was last in Bermuda and had forgotten to mail them. "Would you get those things, darling?" he asked. "Do you remember where we put them?" Then she came back into the room with five or six large and expensive-looking packages and unloaded them into my lap.

I think of my children mostly with delight, and I love to give them presents. I was charmed. It was a ruse, of course— hers, I guessed—and one of many that she must have thought up over the last year to hold their world together. (The wrappings were not fresh, I could see, and when I got home and found in them some old cashmere sweaters that Gil's daughters had not taken to college and a Scotch cap with a soiled sweatband, it only deepened my feeling of sympathy for the Bucknams in their trouble.) With a lap full of presents for my kiddies and sympathy leaking out of every joint, I couldn't give him the ax. We talked about the

5

World Series and about some small matters at the office, and when the rain and the wind began, I helped Mrs. Bucknam shut the windows in the apartment, and then I left and took an early train home through the storm. Five days later, Gil Bucknam went on the wagon for good, and came back to the office to sit again at the right hand of the old man, and my skin was one of the first he went after. It seemed to me that if it had been my destiny to be a Russian ballet dancer, or to make art jewelry, or to paint *Schuhplattler* dancers on bureau drawers and landscapes on clamshells and live in some very low-tide place like Provincetown, I wouldn't have known a queerer bunch of men and women than I knew in the para-blendeum industry, and I decided to strike out on my own.

My mother taught me never to speak about money when there was a shirtful, and I've always been very reluctant to speak about it when there was any scarcity, so I cannot paint much of a picture of what ensued in the next six months. I rented office space—a cubicle with a desk and a phone was what it amounted to—and sent out letters, but the letters were seldom answered and the telephone might just as well have been disconnected, and when it came time to borrow money, I had nowhere to turn. My mother hated Christina, and I don't think she can have much money, in any case, because she never bought me an overcoat or a cheese sand-wich when I was a kid without telling me that it came out of her principal. I had plenty of friends, but if my life depended on it I couldn't ask a man for a drink and touch him for five hundred—and I needed more. The worst of it was that I hadn't painted anything like an adequate picture to my wife.

I thought about this one night when we were dressing to go to dinner up the road at the Warburtons'. Christina was sitting at her dressing table putting on earrings. She is a pretty woman in the prime of life, and her ignorance of financial necessity is complete. Her neck is graceful, her breasts gleamed as they rose in the cloth of her dress, and, seeing the decent and healthy delight she took in her own image, I could not tell her that we were broke. She had sweetened much of my life, and to watch her seemed to freshen the well-springs of some clear energy in me that made the room and the pictures on the wall and the moon that I could see outside the window all vivid and cheerful. The truth would make her cry and ruin her make-up and the Warburtons' dinner party for her, and she would sleep in the guest room. There seemed to be as much truth in her beauty and the power she exerted over my senses as there was in the fact that we were over-drawn at the bank.

The Warburtons are rich, but they don't mix; they may not even care. She is an aging mouse, and he is the kind of man that you wouldn't have liked at school. He has a bad skin and a rasping voice and a fixed idea—lechery. The Warburtons are always spending money, and that's what you talk about with them. The floor of their front hall is black-and-white marble from the old Ritz, and their cabañas at Sea Island are being winterized, and they are flying to Davos for ten days, and buying a pair of saddle horses, and building a new wing. We were late that night, and the Meserves and the Chesneys were already there, but Carl Warburton hadn't come home, and Sheila was worried. "Carl has to walk through a terrible slum to get to the station," she said, "and

7

he carries thousands of dollars on him, and I'm so afraid he'll be *victimized*. . . ." Then Carl came home and told a dirty story to the mixed company, and we went in to dinner. It was the kind of party where everybody has taken a shower and put on their best clothes, and where some old cook has been peeling mushrooms or picking the meat out of crab shells since daybreak. I wanted to have a good time. That was my wish, but my wishes could not get me off the ground that night. I felt as if I was at some God-awful birthday party of my childhood that my mother had brought me to with threats and promises. The party broke up at about half past eleven, and we went home. I stayed out in the garden finishing one of Carl Warburton's cigars. It was a Thursday night, and my checks wouldn't bounce until Tuesday, but I had to do something soon. When I went upstairs, Christina was asleep, and I fell asleep myself, but I woke again at about three.

I had been dreaming about wrapping bread in colored parablendeum Filmex. I had dreamed a full-page spread in a national magazine: BRING SOME COLOR INTO YOUR BREADBOX! The page was covered with jewel-toned loaves of bread— turquoise bread, ruby bread, and bread the color of emeralds. In my sleep the idea had seemed to me like a good one; it had cheered me, and it was a letdown to find myself in the dark bedroom. Feeling sad then, I thought about all the loose ends of my life, and this brought me around to my old mother, who lives alone in a hotel in Cleveland. I saw her getting dressed to go down and have dinner in the hotel dining room. She seemed pitiable, as I imagined her—lonely and among strangers. And yet, when she turned her head, I saw that she still had some biting teeth left in her gums.

She sent me through college, arranged for me to spend my vacations in pleasant landscapes, and fired my ambitions, such as they are, but she bitterly opposed my marriage, and our relations have been strained ever since. I've often invited her to come and live with us, but she always refuses, and always with bad feeling. I send her flowers and presents, and write her every week, but these attentions only seem to fortify her conviction that my marriage was a disaster for her and for me. Then I thought about her apron strings, for when I was a kid, she seemed to be a woman whose apron strings were thrown across the Atlantic and the Pacific Oceans; they seemed to be looped, like vapor trails, across the very drum of Heaven. I thought of her now without rebellion or anxiety —only with sorrow that all our exertions should have been rewarded with so little clear emotion, and that we could not drink a cup of tea together without stirring up all kinds of bitter feeling. I longed to correct this, to re-enact the whole relationship with my mother against a more simple and human background, where the cost of my education would not have come so high in morbid emotion. I wanted to do it all over again in some emotional Arcadia, and have us both behave differently, so that I could think of her at three in the morning without guilt, and so that she would be spared loneliness and neglect in her old age.

I moved a little closer to Christina and, coming into the area of her warmth, suddenly felt all kindly and delighted with everything, but she moved in her sleep, away from me. Then I coughed. I coughed again. I coughed loudly. I couldn't stop coughing, and I got out of bed and went into the dark bathroom and drank a glass of water. I stood at the bathroom window and looked down into the garden. There was a little wind. It seemed to be changing its quarter. It sounded like a dawn wind—the air was filled with a showery sound—and felt good on my face. There were some cigarettes on the back of the toilet, and I lit one in order to get back to sleep. But when I inhaled the smoke, it hurt my lungs, and I was suddenly convinced that I was dying of bronchial cancer.

I have experienced all kinds of foolish melancholy—I've been homesick for countries I've never seen, and longed to be what I couldn't be—but all these moods were trivial compared to my premonition of death. I tossed my cigarette into the toilet (ping) and straightened my back, but the pain in my chest was only sharper, and I was convinced that the corruption had begun. I had friends who would think of me kindly, I knew, and Christina and the children would surely keep alive an affectionate memory. But then I thought about money again, and the Warburtons, and my rubber checks approaching the clearing house, and it seemed to me that money had it all over love. I have yearned for some women —turned green, in fact—but it seemed to me that I had never yearned for anyone the way I yearned that night for money. I went to the closet in our bedroom and put on some old blue sneakers and a pair of pants and a dark pullover. Then I went downstairs and out of the house. The moon had set, and there were not many stars, but the air above the trees and hedges was full of dim light. I went around the Trenholmes' garden then, gumshoeing over the grass, and down the lawn to the Warburtons' house. I listened for sounds from the open windows, and all I heard was the ticking of a clock. I went up the front steps and opened the screen door and started across the floor from the old Ritz. In the dim night light that came in at the windows, the house looked like a shell, a nautilus, shaped to contain itself.

I heard the noise of a dog's license tag, and Sheila's old cocker came trotting down the hall. I rubbed him behind the ears, and then he went back to wherever his bed was, grunted, and fell asleep. I knew the plan of the Warburtons' house as well as I knew the plan of my own. The staircase was carpeted, but I first put my foot on one of the treads to see if it creaked. Then I started up the stairs. All the bedroom doors stood open, and from Carl and Sheila's bedroom, where I had often left my coat at big cocktail parties, I could hear the sound of deep breathing. I stood in the doorway for a second to take my bearings. In the dimness I could see the bed, and a pair of pants and a jacket hung over the back of a chair. Moving swiftly, I stepped into the room and took a big billfold from the inside pocket of the coat and started back to the hall. The violence of my emotion may have made me clumsy, because Sheila woke. I heard her say, "Did you hear that noise, darling?" "S'wind," he mumbled, and then they were quiet again. I was safe in the hall—safe from everything but myself. I seemed to be having a nervous breakdown out there. All my saliva was gone, the lubricants seemed to drain out of my heart, and whatever the juices were that kept my legs upright were going. It was only by holding on to the wall that I could make any progress at all. I clung to the banister on my way down the stairs, and staggered out of the house.

Back in my own dark kitchen, I drank three or four glasses of water. I must have stood by the kitchen sink for a half hour or longer before I thought of looking in Carl's wallet. I went into the cellarway and shut the cellar door before I turned the light on. There was a little over nine hundred dollars. I turned the light off and went back into the dark kitchen. Oh, I never knew that a man could be so miserable and that the mind could open up so many chambers and fill them with self-reproach! Where were the trout streams of my youth, and other innocent pleasures? The wet-leather smell of the loud waters and the keen woods after a smashing rain; or at opening day the summer breezes smelling like the grassy breath of Holsteins—your head would swim—and all the brooks full then (or so I imagined, in the dark kitchen) of trout, our sunken treasure. I was crying.

Shady Hill is, as I say, a *banlieue* and open to criticism by city planners, adventurers, and lyric poets, but if you work in the city and have children to raise, I can't think of a better place. My neighbors are rich, it is true, but riches in this case mean leisure, and they use their time wisely. They travel around the world, listen to good music, and, given a choice of paper books at an airport, will pick Thucydides, and sometimes Aquinas. Urged to build bomb shelters, they plant trees and roses, and their gardens are splendid and bright. Had I looked, the next morning, from my bathroom window into the evil-smelling ruin of some great city, the shock of recalling what I had done might not have been so violent, but the moral bottom had dropped out of my world without changing a mote of sunlight. I dressed stealthily—for what child of darkness would want to hear the merry voices of his family?—and caught an early train. My gabardine suit was meant to express cleanliness and probity, but I was a miserable creature whose footsteps had been mistaken for the noise of the wind. I looked at the paper. There had been a thirty-thousand-dollar payroll robbery in the Bronx. A White Plains matron had come home from a party to find her furs and jewelry gone. Sixty thousand dollars' worth of medicine had been taken from a warehouse in Brooklyn. I felt better at discovering how common the thing I had done was. But only a little better, and only for a short while. Then I was faced once more with the realization that I was a common thief and an impostor, and that I had done something so reprehensible that it violated the tenets of every known religion. I had stolen, and what's more, I had criminally entered the house of a friend and broken all the unwritten laws that held the community together. My conscience worked so on my spirits—like the hard beak of a carnivorous bird—that my left eye began to twitch, and again I seemed on the brink of a general nervous collapse. When the train reached the city, I went to the bank. Leaving the bank, I was nearly hit by a taxi. My anxiety was not for my bones but for the fact that Carl Warburton's wallet might be found in my pocket. When I thought no one was looking, I wiped the wallet on my trousers (to remove the fingerprints) and dropped it into an ash can.

I thought that coffee might make me feel better, and went into a restaurant, and sat down at a table with a stranger. The soiled lace-paper doilies and half-empty glasses of water had not been taken away, and at the stranger's place there was a thirty-five-cent tip, left by an earlier customer. I looked at the menu, but out of the corner of my eye I saw the stranger pocket the thirty-five-cent tip. What a crook! I got up and left the restaurant.

I walked to my cubicle, hung up my hat and coat, sat down

13

at my desk, shot my cuffs, sighed, and looked into space, as if a day full of challenge and decision were about to begin. I hadn't turned on the light. In a little while, the office beside mine was occupied, and I heard my neighbor clear his throat, cough, scratch a match, and settle down to attack the day's business.

The walls were flimsy—part frosted glass and part plywood—and there was no acoustical privacy in these offices. I reached into my pocket for a cigarette with as much stealth as I had exercised at the Warburtons', and waited for the noise of a truck passing on the street outside before I lit a match. The excitement of eavesdropping took hold of me. My neighbor was trying to sell uranium stock over the telephone. His line went like this: First he was courteous. Then he was nasty. "What's the matter, Mr. X? Don't you want to make any money?" Then he was *very* scornful. "I'm sorry to have bothered you, Mr. X. I thought you *had* sixty-five dollars to invest." He called twelve numbers without any takers. I was as quiet as a mouse. Then he telephoned the information desk at Idlewild, checking the arrival of planes from Europe. London was on time. Rome and Paris were late. "No, he ain't in yet," I heard him say to someone over the phone. "It's dark in there." My heart was beating fast. Then my telephone began to ring, and I counted twelve rings before it stopped. "I'm positive, I'm positive," the man in the next office said. "I can hear his telephone ringing, and he ain't answering it, and he's just a lonely son of a bitch looking for a job. Go ahead, go ahead, I tell you. I ain't got time to get over there. Go ahead. . . . Seven, eight, three, five, seven, seven. . . ." When he hung up, I went to the door, opened and closed it, turned the light on, rattled the coat hangers, whistled a tune, sat down heavily at my desk chair, and dialed the first telephone number that came to my mind. It was an old friend—Burt Howe—and he exclaimed when he heard my voice. "Hakie, I been looking for you everywhere! You sure folded up your tents and stole away."

"Yes," I said.

"Stole away," Howe repeated. "Just stole away. But what I wanted to talk with you about is this deal I thought you might be interested in. It's a one-shot, but it won't take you more than three weeks. It's a steal. They're green, and they're dumb, and they're loaded, and it's just like stealing."

"Yes," I said.

"Well, then, can you meet me for lunch at Cardin's at twelve-thirty, and I'll give you the details?" Howe asked.

"O.K.," I said hoarsely. "Thanks a lot, Burt."

"We went out to the shack on Sunday," the man in the next office was saying as I hung up. "Louise got bit by a poisonous spider. The doctor gave her some kind of injection. She'll be all right." He dialed another number and said, "We went out to the shack on Sunday. Louise got bit by a poisonous spider. The doctor gave her some kind of injection. She'll be all right." He dialed another number and began, "We went out to the shack on Sunday. Louise got bit by a poisonous spider . . ."

It was possible that a man whose wife had been bitten by a spider and who found some time on his hands might call three or four friends and tell them about it, and it was equally possible that the spider might be a code of warning or of assent to some unlawful traffic. What frightened me was that by becoming a thief I seemed to have surrounded myself with thieves and operators. My left eye had begun to twitch again, and the inability of one part of my consciousness to stand up under the reproach that was being heaped onto it by another part made me cast around desperately for someone else who could be blamed. I had read often enough in the papers that divorce sometimes led to crime. My parents were divorced when I was about five. This was a good clue and quickly led me on to something better.

My father went to live in France after the divorce, and I didn't see him for ten years. Then he wrote Mother for permission to see me, and she prepared me for this reunion by telling me how drunken, cruel, and lewd the old man was. It was in the summer, and we were on Nantucket, and I took the steamer alone, and went to New York on the train. I met my father at the Plaza early in the evening, but not so early that he hadn't begun to drink. With the long, sensitive nose of an adolescent I smelled the gin on his breath, and I noticed that he bumped into a table and sometimes repeated himself. I realized later that this reunion must have been strenuous for a man of sixty, which he was. We had dinner and then went to see *The Roses of Picardy*. As soon as the chorus came on, Father said that I could have any one of them that I wanted; the arrangements were all made. I could even have one of the specialty dancers. Now, if I'd felt that he had crossed the Atlantic to perform this service for me, it might have been different, but I felt he'd made the trip in order to do a disservice to my mother. I was scared. The show was in one of those old-fashioned theaters that appear to be held together with angels. Brown-gold angels held up the ceiling; they held up the boxes; they even seemed to hold up the balcony with about four hundred people in it. I spent a lot of time looking at those dusty gold angels. If the ceiling of the theater had fallen on my head, I would have been relieved. After the show, we went back to the hotel to wash before meeting the girls, and the old man stretched out on the bed for a minute and began to snore. I picked his wallet of fifty dollars, spent the night in Grand Central, and took an early-morning train to Woods Hole. So the whole thing was explained, including the violence of the emotion I had experienced in the Warburtons' upstairs hall; I had been re-living that scene at the Plaza. It had not been my fault that I had stolen then, and it had not been my fault when I went to the Warburtons'. It was my father's fault! Then I remem-bered that my father was buried in Fontainebleau fifteen years ago, and could be nothing much more now than dust.

I went into the men's room and washed my hands and face, and combed my hair down with a lot of water. It was time to go out for lunch. I thought anxiously of the lunch ahead of me, and, wondering why, was astonished to realize that it was Burt Howe's free use of the word "steal." I hoped he wouldn't keep on saying it.

Even as the thought floated across my mind in the men's room, the twitching in my eye seemed to spread over my cheek; it seemed as if this verb were embedded in the English language like a poisoned fishhook. I had committed adultery, and the word "adultery" had no force for me; I had been drunk, and the word "drunkenness" had no extraordinary power. It was only "steal" and all its allied nouns, verbs, and

17

adverbs that had the power to tyrannize over my nervous system, as if I had evolved, unconsciously, some doctrine wherein the act of theft took precedence over all the other sins in the Decalogue and was a sign of moral death.

The sky was dark when I came out on the street. Lights were burning everywhere. I looked into the faces of the people that I passed for some encouraging signs of honesty in such a crooked world, and on Third Avenue I saw a young man with a tin cup, holding his eyes shut to impersonate blindness. That seal of blindness, the striking innocence of the upper face, was betrayed by the frown and the crow's-feet of a man who could see his drinks on the bar. There was another blind beggar on Forty-first Street, but I didn't examine his eye sockets, realizing that I couldn't assess the legitimacy of every beggar in the city.

Cardin's is a men's restaurant in the Forties. The stir and bustle in the vestibule only made me feel retiring, and the hat-check girl, noticing, I suppose, the twitch in my eye, gave me a very jaded look.

Burt was at the bar, and when we had ordered our drinks, we got down to business. "For a deal like this, we ought to meet in some back alley," he said, "but a fool and his money *and* so forth. It's three kids. P. J. Burdette is one of them, and they've got a cool million between them to throw away. Someone's bound to steal from them, so it may as well be you." I put my hand over the left side of my face to cover the tic. When I tried to raise my glass to my mouth, I spilled gin all over my suit. "They're all three of them just out of college," Burt said. "And they've all three of them got so much in the kitty that even if you picked them clean they wouldn't feel any pain. Now, in order to participate in this burglary, all you have to do . . ."

The toilet was at the other end of the restaurant, but I got there. Then I drew a basin of cold water and stuck my head and face into it. Burt had followed me into the washroom. As I was drying myself with a paper towel, he said, "You know, Hakie, I wasn't going to mention it, but now that you've been sick, I may as well tell you that you look awful. I mean from the minute I saw you I knew something was wrong. I just want to tell you that whatever it is—sauce or dope or trouble at home—it's a lot later than you think, and maybe you should be doing something about it. No hard feelings?" I said that I was sick, and waited in the toilet long enough for Burt to make a getaway. Then I got my hat and another jaded look from the hat-check girl, and saw in the afternoon paper on a chair by the checkroom that some bank robbers in Brooklyn had got away with eighteen thousand dollars.

I walked around the streets, wondering how I would shape up as a pickpocket and bag snatcher, and all the arches and spires of St. Patrick's only reminded me of poor boxes. I took the regular train home, looking out of the window at a peaceable landscape and a spring evening, and it seemed to me that fishermen and lone bathers and grade-crossing watchmen and sand-lot ballplayers and lovers unashamed of their sport and the owners of small sailing craft and old men playing pinochle in firehouses were the people who stitched up the big holes in the world that were made by men like me.

Now, Christina is the kind of woman who, when she is asked by the alumnae secretary of her college to describe her status, gets dizzy thinking about the variety of her activities and interests. And what, on a given day, stretching a point here and there, does she have to do? Drive me to the train. Have the skis repaired. Book a tennis court. Buy the wine and groceries for the monthly dinner of the Société Gastronomique du Westchester Nord. Look up some definitions in Larousse. Attend a League of Women Voters symposium on sewers. Go to a full-dress lunch for Bobsie Neil's aunt. Weed the garden. Iron a uniform for the part-time maid. Type two and a half pages of her paper on the early novels of Henry James. Empty the wastebaskets. Help Tabitha prepare the children's supper. Give Ronnie some batting practice. Put her hair in pin curls. Get the cook. Meet the train. Bathe. Dress. Greet her guests in French at half past seven. Say *bon soir* at eleven. Lie in my arms until twelve. Eureka! You might say that she is prideful, but I think only that she is a woman enjoying herself in a country that is prosperous and young. Still, when she met me at the train that night, it was difficult for me to rise to all this vitality.

It was my bad luck to have to take the collection at early Communion on Sunday, although I was in no condition. I answered the pious looks of my friends with a very crooked smile and then knelt by a lancet-shaped stained-glass window that seemed to be made from the butts of vermouth and Burgundy bottles. I knelt on an imitation-leather hassock that had been given by some guild or auxiliary to replace one of the old, snuff-colored hassocks, which had begun to split at the seams and show bits of straw, and made the whole place smell like an old manger. The smell of straw and flowers, and the vigil light, and the candles flickering in the rector's breath, and the damp of this poorly heated stone building were all as familiar to me and belonged as much to my early life as the sounds and smells of a kitchen or a nursery, and yet they seemed, that morning, to be so potent that I felt dizzy. Then I heard, in the baseboard on my right, a rat's tooth working like an auger in the hard oak. "Holy, Holy, Holy," I said, very loudly, hoping to frighten the rat. "Lord God of hosts, Heaven and earth are FULL of Thy Glory!" The small congregation muttered its amens with a sound like a footstep, and the rat went on scraping away at the baseboard. And then—perhaps because I was absorbed in the noise of the rat's tooth, or because the smell of dampness and straw was soporific—when I looked up from the shelter I had made of my hands, I saw the rector drinking from the chalice and realized that I had missed Communion.

At home, I looked through the Sunday paper for other thefts, and there were plenty. Banks had been looted, hotel safes had been emptied of jewelry, maids and butlers had been tied to kitchen chairs, furs and industrial diamonds had been stolen in job lots, delicatessens, cigar stores, and pawnshops had been broken into, and someone had stolen a painting from the Cleveland Institute of Art. Late in the afternoon, I raked leaves. What could be more contrite than cleaning the lawn of the autumn's dark rubbish under the streaked, pale skies of spring?

While I was raking leaves, my sons walked by. "The Toblers are having a softball game," Ronnie said. "*Everybody's* there."

"Why don't you play?" I asked.

21

"You can't play unless you've been invited," Ronnie said over his shoulder, and then they were gone. Then I noticed that I could hear the cheering from the softball game to which we had not been invited. The Toblers lived down the block. The spirited voices seemed to sound clearer and clearer as the night came on; I could even hear the noise of ice in glasses, and the voices of the ladies raised in a feeble cheer.

Why hadn't I been asked to play softball at the Toblers', I wondered. Why had we been excluded from these simple pleasures, this lighthearted gathering, the fading laughter and voices and slammed doors of which seemed to gleam in the darkness as they were withdrawn from my possession? Why wasn't *I* asked to play softball at the Toblers'? Why should social aggrandizement—*climbing*, really—exclude a nice guy like me from a softball game? What kind of a world was that? Why should I be left alone with my dead leaves in the twilight—as I was—feeling so forsaken, lonely, and forlorn that I was chilled?

If there is anybody I detest, it is weak-minded sentimental-ists—all those melancholy people who, out of an excess of sympathy for others, miss the thrill of their own essence and drift through life without identity, like a human fog, feeling sorry for everyone. The legless beggar in Times Square with his poor display of pencils, the rouged old lady in the subway who talks to herself, the exhibitionist in the public toilet, the drunk who has dropped on the subway stairs do more than excite their pity; they are at a glance transformed into these unfortunates. Derelict humanity seems to trample over their unrealized souls, leaving them at twilight in a condition closely resembling the scene of a prison riot. Disappointed in themselves, they are always ready to be disappointed for the rest of us, and they will build whole cities, whole creations, firmaments and principalities, of tear-wet disappointment. Lying in bed at night, they will think tenderly of the big winner who lost his pari-mutuel ticket, of the great novelist whose magnum opus was burned mistakenly for trash, and of Samuel Tilden, who lost the Presidency of the United States through the shenanigans of the electoral college. Detesting this company, then, it was doubly painful for me to find myself in it. And, seeing a bare dogwood tree in the starlight, I thought, How sad everything is!

Wednesday was my birthday. I recalled this fact in the middle of the afternoon, at the office, and the thought that Christina might be planning a surprise party brought me in one second from a sitting to a standing position, breathless. Then I decided that she wouldn't. But just the preparations the children would make presented an emotional problem; I didn't see how I could face it.

I left the office early and had two drinks before I took the train. Christina looked pleased with everything when she met me at the station, and I put a very good face on my anxiety. The children had changed into clean clothes, and wished me a happy birthday so fervently that I felt awful. At the table there was a pile of small presents, mostly things that the children had made—cuff links out of buttons, and a memo pad, and so forth. I thought I was very bright, considering the circumstances, and pulled my snapper, put on

23

my silly hat, blew out the candles on the cake, and thanked them all, but then it seemed that there was another present —my *big* present—and after dinner I was made to stay inside while Christina and the children went outside, and then Juney came in and led me outdoors and around in back of the house, where they all were. Leaning against the house was an aluminum extension ladder with a card and a ribbon tied to it, and I said, as if I'd been hit, "What in *hell* is the meaning of this?"

"We thought you'd need it, Daddy," Juney said.

"What would I ever need a ladder for? What do you think I am—a second-story worker?"

"Storm windows," Juney said. "Screens—"

I turned to Christina. "Have I been talking in my sleep?"

"No," Christina said. "You haven't been talking in your sleep."

Juney began to cry.

"You could take the leaves out of the rain gutters," Ronnie said. Both of the boys were looking at me with long faces.

"Well, you must admit it's a very unusual present," I said to Christina.

"*God!*" Christina said. "Come on, children. Come on." She herded them in at the terrace door.

I kicked around the garden until after dark. The lights went on upstairs. Juney was still crying, and Christina was singing to her. Then she was quiet. I waited until the lights went on in our bedroom, and after a little while I climbed the stairs. Christina was in a nightgown, sitting at her dressing table, and there were heavy tears in her eyes.

"You'll have to try and understand," I said.

"I couldn't possibly. The children have been saving for months to buy you that damned-fool contraption."

"You don't know what I've been through," I said.

"If you'd been through hell, I wouldn't forgive you," she said. "You haven't been through anything that would justify your behavior. They've had it hidden in the garage for a week. They're so *sweet*."

"I haven't felt like myself," I said.

"Don't tell *me* that you haven't felt like yourself," she said. "I've looked forward to having you leave in the morning, and I've dreaded having you come home at night."

"It can't have been all that bad," I said.

"It's been hell," she said. "You've been sharp with the children, nasty to me, rude to your friends, and malicious behind their backs. It's been hideous."

"Would you like me to go?"

"Oh, Lord, would I like you to go! Then I could breathe."

"What about the children?"

"Ask my lawyer."

"I'll go, then."

I went down the hall to the closet where we keep the bags. When I took out my suitcase, I found that the children's puppy had chewed the leather binding loose all along one side. Trying to find another suitcase, I brought the whole pile down on top of me, boxing my ears. I carried my bag with this long strip of leather trailing behind me back into our bedroom. "*Look*," I said. "Look at this, Christina. The dog has chewed the binding off my suitcase." She didn't even raise her head. "I've poured twenty thousand dollars a year into this establishment for ten years," I shouted, "and when the time comes for me to go, I don't even have a decent suit-case! Everybody else has a suitcase. Even the cat has a nice traveling bag." I threw open my shirt drawer, and there were only four clean shirts. "I don't have enough clean shirts to last a week!" I shouted. Then I got a few things together, clapped my hat on my head, and marched out. I even thought, for a minute, of taking the car, and I went into the garage and looked it over. Then I saw the FOR SALE sign that had been hanging on the house when we bought it long, long ago. I wiped the dirt off the sign and got a nail and a rock and went around to the front of the house and nailed the FOR SALE sign onto a maple tree. Then I walked to the station. It's about a mile. The long strip of leather was trailing along behind me, and I stopped and tried to rip it off the suitcase, but it wouldn't come. When I got down to the station, I found there wasn't another train until four in the morning. I decided I would wait. I sat down on my suitcase and waited five minutes. Then I marched home again. Halfway there I saw Christina coming down the street, in a sweater and a skirt and sneakers—the quickest things to put on, but sum-mery things—and we walked home together and went to bed.

On Saturday, I played golf, and although the game finished late, I wanted to take a swim in the club pool before I went home. There was no one at the pool but Tom Maitland. He is a dark-skinned and nice-looking man, very rich, but quiet. He seems withdrawn. His wife is the fattest woman in Shady Hill, and nobody much likes his children, and I think he is the kind of man whose parties and friendships and affairs in love and business all rest like an intricate superstructure—a tower of matchsticks—on the melancholy of his early youth. A breath could bring the whole thing down. It was nearly dark when I had finished swimming; the club house was lighted and you could hear the sounds of dinner from the porch. Maitland was sitting at the edge of the pool dabbling his feet in the bright-blue water, with its Dead Sea smell of chlorine. I was drying myself off, and as I passed him, I asked if he wasn't going in. "I don't know how to swim," he said. He smiled and looked away from me then to the still-polished water of the pool, in the dark landscape. "We used to have a pool at home," he said, "but I never got a chance to swim in it. I was always studying the violin." There he was, forty-five years old and at least a millionaire, and he couldn't even float, and I don't suppose he had many occasions to speak as honestly as he had just spoken. While I was getting dressed, the idea settled in my head—with no help from me—that the Maitlands would be my next victims.

A few nights later, I woke up at three. I thought over the loose ends in my life—Mother in Cleveland, and parablendeum—and then I went into the bathroom to light a cigarette before I remembered that I was dying of bronchial cancer and leaving my widow and orphans penniless. I put on my blue sneakers and the rest of the outfit, looked in at the open doors of the children's rooms, and then went out. It was cloudy. I walked through back gardens to the corner. Then I crossed the street and turned up the Maitlands' driveway, walking on the grass at the edge of the gravel. The door was open, and I went in, just as excited and frightened as I had been at the Warburtons', and feeling insubstantial in the dim light—a ghost. I followed my nose up the stairs to where I knew their bedroom was, and, hearing heavy breathing and seeing a jacket and some pants on a chair, I reached for the pocket of the jacket, but there wasn't one. It wasn't a suit coat at all; it was one of those bright satin jackets that kids wear. There was no sense in looking for a wallet in *his* trousers. He couldn't make that much cutting the Maitlands' grass. I got out of there in a hurry.

I did not sleep any more that night but sat in the dark thinking about Tom Maitland, and Gracie Maitland, and the Warburtons, and Christina, and my own sordid destiny, and how different Shady Hill looked at night than in the light of day.

But I went out the next night—this time to the Pewters', who were not only rich but booze fighters, and who drank so much that I didn't see how they could hear thunder after the lights were turned out. I left, as usual, a little after three.

I was thinking sadly about my beginnings—about how I was made by a riggish couple in a midtown hotel after a six-course dinner with wines, and my mother had told me many times that if she hadn't drunk so many Old-Fashioneds before that famous dinner I would still be unborn on a star. And I thought about my old man and that night at the Plaza and the bruised thighs of the peasant women of Picardy and all the brown-gold angels that held the theater together and my terrible destiny. While I was walking toward the Pewters', there was a harsh stirring in all the trees and gardens, like a draft on a bed of fire, and I wondered what it was until I felt the rain on my hands and face, and then I began to laugh.

I wish I could say that a kindly lion had set me straight, or an innocent child, or the strains of distant music from some church, but it was no more than the rain on my head—the smell of it flying up to my nose—that showed me the extent of my freedom from the bones in Fontainebleau and the works of a thief. There were ways out of my trouble if I cared to make use of them. I was not trapped. I was here on earth because I chose to be. And it was no skin off my elbow how I had been given the gifts of life so long as I possessed them, and I possessed them then—the tie between the wet grass roots and the hair that grew out of my body, the thrill of my mortality that I had known on summer nights, loving the children, and looking down the front of Christina's dress. I was standing in front of the Pewters' by this time, and I looked up at the dark house and then turned and walked away. I went back to bed and had pleasant dreams. I dreamed I was sailing a boat on the Mediterranean. I saw some worn marble steps leading down into the water, and the water itself —blue, saline, and dirty. I stepped the mast, hoisted the sail, and put my hand on the tiller. But why, I wondered as I sailed away, should I seem to be only seventeen years old? But you can't have everything.

It is not, as somebody once wrote, the smell of corn bread that calls us back from death; it is the lights and signs of love and friendship. Gil Bucknam called me the next day and said that the old man was dying and would I come back to work? I went to see him, and he explained that it was the old man who was after my skin, and, of course, I was glad to come home to parablendeum.

What I did not understand, as I walked down Fifth Avenue that afternoon, was how a world that had seemed so dark could, in a few minutes, become so sweet. The sidewalks seemed to shine, and, going home on the train, I beamed at those foolish girls who advertise girdles on the signboards in the Bronx. I got an advance on my salary the next morning, and, taking some precautions about fingerprints, I put nine hundred dollars into an envelope and walked over to the Warburtons' when the last lights in the neighborhood had been put out. It had been raining, but the rain had let up. The stars were beginning to show. There was no sense in overdoing prudence, and I went around to the back of their house, found the kitchen door open, and put the envelope on a table in the dark room. As I was walking away from the house, a police car drew up beside me, and a patrolman I knew cranked down the window and asked, "What are you doing out at this time of night, Mr. Hake?"

"I'm walking the dog," I said cheerfully. There was no dog in sight, but they didn't look. "Here, Toby! Here, Toby! Here, Toby! *Good* dog!" I called, and off I went, whistling merrily in the dark.

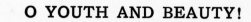

O YOUTH AND BEAUTY!

✳   **AT THE TAG END** of nearly every long, large Saturday-night party in the suburb of Shady Hill, when almost everybody who was going to play golf or tennis in the morning had gone home hours ago and the ten or twelve people remaining seemed powerless to bring the evening to an end although the gin and whiskey were running low, and here and there a woman who was sitting out her husband would have begun to drink milk; when everybody had lost track of time, and the baby sitters who were waiting at home for these diehards would have long since stretched out on the sofa and fallen into a deep sleep, to dream about cooking-contest prizes, ocean voyages, and romance; when the bellicose drunk, the crapshooter, the pianist, and the woman faced with the expiration of her hopes had all expressed themselves; when every proposal—to go to the Farquarsons' for breakfast, to go swimming, to go and wake up the Townsends, to go here and go there—died as soon as it was made, then Trace Bearden would begin to chide Cash Bentley about his age and thinning hair. The chiding was preliminary to moving the living-room furniture. Trace and Cash moved

33

the tables and the chairs, the sofas and the fire screen, the woodbox and the footstool; and when they had finished, you wouldn't know the place. Then if the host had a revolver, he would be asked to produce it. Cash would take off his shoes and assume a starting crouch behind a sofa. Trace would fire the weapon out of an open window, and if you were new to the community and had not understood what the preparations were about, you would then realize that you were watching a hurdle race. Over the sofa went Cash, over the tables, over the fire screen and the woodbox. It was not exactly a race, since Cash ran it alone, but it was extraordinary to see this man of forty surmount so many obstacles so gracefully. There was not a piece of furniture in Shady Hill that Cash could not take in his stride. The race ended with cheers, and presently the party would break up.

Cash was, of course, an old track star, but he was never aggressive or tiresome about his brilliant past. The college where he had spent his youth had offered him a paying job on the alumni council, but he had refused it, realizing that that part of his life was ended. Cash and his wife, Louise, had two children, and they lived in a medium-cost ranchhouse on Alewives Lane. They belonged to the country club, although they could not afford it, but in the case of the Bentleys nobody ever pointed this out, and Cash was one of the best-liked men in Shady Hill. He was still slender—he was careful about his weight—and he walked to the train in the morning with a light and vigorous step that marked him as an athlete. His hair was thin, and there were mornings when his eyes looked bloodshot, but this did not detract much from a charming quality of stubborn youthfulness.

In business Cash had suffered reverses and disappointments, and the Bentleys had many money worries. They were always late with their tax payments and their mortgage payments, and the drawer of the hall table was stuffed with unpaid bills; it was always touch and go with the Bentleys and the bank. Louise looked pretty enough on Saturday night, but her life was exacting and monotonous. In the pockets of her suits, coats, and dresses there were little wads and scraps of paper on which was written: "Oleomargarine, frozen spinach, Kleenex, dog biscuit, hamburger, pepper, lard . . ." When she was still half awake in the morning, she was putting on the water for coffee and diluting the frozen orange juice. Then she would be wanted by the children. She would crawl under the bureau on her hands and knees to find a sock for Toby. She would lie flat on her belly and wriggle under the bed (getting dust up her nose) to find a shoe for Rachel. Then there were the housework, the laundry, and the cooking, as well as the demands of the children. There always seemed to be shoes to put on and shoes to take off, snowsuits to be zipped and unzipped, bottoms to be wiped, tears to be dried, and when the sun went down (she saw it set from the kitchen window) there was the supper to be cooked, the baths, the bedtime story, and the Lord's Prayer. With the sonorous words of the Our Father in a darkened room the children's day was over, but the day was far from over for Louise Bentley. There were the darning, the mending, and some ironing to do, and after sixteen years of housework she did not seem able to escape her chores even while she slept. Snowsuits, shoes, baths, and groceries seemed to have permeated her subconscious. Now and then she would

35

speak in her sleep—so loudly that she woke her husband. "I can't *afford* veal cutlets," she said one night. Then she sighed uneasily and was quiet again.

By the standards of Shady Hill, the Bentleys were a happily married couple, but they had their ups and downs. Cash could be very touchy at times. When he came home after a bad day at the office and found that Louise, for some good reason, had not started supper, he would be ugly. "Oh, for Christ sake!" he would say, and go into the kitchen and heat up some frozen food. He drank some whiskey to relax himself during this ordeal, but it never seemed to relax him, and he usually burned the bottom out of a pan, and when they sat down for supper the dining space would be full of smoke. It was only a question of time before they were plunged into a bitter quarrel. Louise would run upstairs, throw herself onto the bed, and sob. Cash would grab the whiskey bottle and dose himself. These rows, in spite of the vigor with which Cash and Louise entered into them, were the source of a great deal of pain for both of them. Cash would sleep downstairs on the sofa, but sleep never repaired the damage, once the trouble had begun, and if they met in the morning, they would be at one another's throats in a second. Then Cash would leave for the train, and, as soon as the children had been taken to nursery school, Louise would put on her coat and cross the grass to the Beardens' house. She would cry into a cup of warmed-up coffee and tell Lucy Bearden her troubles. What was the meaning of marriage? What was the meaning of love? Lucy always suggested that Louise get a job. It would give her emotional and financial independence, and that, Lucy said, was what she needed.

The next night, things would get worse. Cash would not come home for dinner at all, but would stumble in at about eleven, and the whole sordid wrangle would be repeated, with Louise going to bed in tears upstairs and Cash again stretching out on the living-room sofa. After a few days and nights of this, Louise would decide that she was at the end of her rope. She would decide to go and stay with her married sister in Mamaroneck. She usually chose a Saturday, when Cash would be at home, for her departure. She would pack a suitcase and get her War Bonds from the desk. Then she would take a bath and put on her best slip. Cash, passing the bedroom door, would see her. Her slip was transparent, and suddenly he was all repentance, tenderness, charm, wisdom, and love. "Oh, my darling!" he would groan, and when they went downstairs to get a bite to eat about an hour later, they would be sighing and making cow eyes at one another; they would be the happiest married couple in the whole Eastern United States. It was usually at about this time that Lucy Bearden turned up with the good news that she had found a job for Louise. Lucy would ring the doorbell, and Cash, wearing a bathrobe, would let her in. She would be brief with Cash, naturally, and hurry into the dining room to tell poor Louise the good news. "Well that's very nice of you to have looked," Louise would say wanly, "but I don't think that I want a job any more. I don't think that Cash wants me to work, do you, sweetheart?" Then she would turn her big dark eyes on Cash, and you could practically smell smoke. Lucy would excuse herself hurriedly from this scene of depravity, but she never left with any hard feelings, because she had been married for nineteen years herself and she knew that every union has its ups and downs. She didn't seem to leave any wiser, either; the next time the Bentleys quarreled, she would be just as intent as ever on getting Louise a job. But these quarrels and reunions, like the hurdle race, didn't seem to lose their interest through repetition.

On a Saturday night in the spring, the Farquarsons gave the Bentleys an anniversary party. It was their seventeenth anniversary. Saturday afternoon, Louise Bentley put herself through preparations nearly as arduous as the Monday wash. She rested for an hour, by the clock, with her feet high in the air, her chin in a sling, and her eyes bathed in some astringent solution. The clay packs, the too tight girdle, and the plucking and curling and painting that went on were all aimed at rejuvenation. Feeling in the end that she had not been entirely successful, she tied a piece of veiling over her eyes—but she was a lovely woman, and all the cosmetics that she had struggled with seemed, like her veil, to be drawn transparently over a face where mature beauty and a capacity for wit and passion were undisguisable. The Farquarsons' party was nifty, and the Bentleys had a wonderful time. The only person who drank too much was Trace Bearden. Late in the party, he began to chide Cash about his thinning hair and Cash good-naturedly began to move the furniture around. Harry Farquarson had a pistol, and Trace went out onto the terrace to fire it up at the sky. Over the sofa went Cash, over the end table, over the arms of the wing chair and the fire screen. It was a piece of carving on a chest that brought him down, and down he came like a ton of bricks.

Louise screamed and ran to where he lay. He had cut a

gash in his forehead, and someone made a bandage to stop the flow of blood. When he tried to get up, he stumbled and fell again, and his face turned a terrible green. Harry telephoned Dr. Parminter, Dr. Hopewell, Dr. Altman, and Dr. Barnstable, but it was two in the morning and none of them answered. Finally, a Dr. Yerkes—a total stranger—agreed to come. Yerkes was a young man—he did not seem old enough to be a doctor—and he looked around at the disordered room and the anxious company as if there was something weird about the scene. He got off on the wrong foot with Cash. "What seems to be the matter, old-timer?" he asked.

Cash's leg was broken. The doctor put a splint on it, and Harry and Trace carried the injured man out to the doctor's car. Louise followed them in her own car to the hospital, where Cash was bedded down in a ward. The doctor gave Cash a sedative, and Louise kissed him and drove home in the dawn.

Cash was in the hospital for two weeks, and when he came home he walked with a crutch and his broken leg was in a heavy cast. It was another ten days before he could limp to the morning train. "I won't be able to run the hurdle race any more, sweetheart," he told Louise sadly. She said that it didn't matter, but while it didn't matter to her, it seemed to matter to Cash. He had lost weight in the hospital. His spirits were low. He seemed discontented. He did not himself understand what had happened. He, or everything around him, seemed subtly to have changed for the worse. Even his senses seemed to conspire to damage the ingenuous world that he had enjoyed for so many years. He went into the kitchen late one night to make himself a sandwich, and when he opened the icebox door he noticed a rank smell. He dumped the spoiled meat into the garbage, but the smell clung to his nostrils. A few days later he was in the attic, looking for his old varsity sweater. There were no windows in the attic and his flashlight was dim. Kneeling on the floor to unlock a trunk, he broke a spider web with his lips. The frail web covered his mouth as if a hand had been put over it. He wiped it impatiently, but also with the feeling of having been gagged. A few nights later, he was walking down a New York side street in the rain and saw an old whore standing in a doorway. She was so sluttish and ugly that she looked like a cartoon of Death, but before he could appraise her—the instant his eyes took an impression of her crooked figure—his lips swelled, his breathing quickened, and he experienced all the other symptoms of erotic excitement. A few nights later, while he was reading *Time* in the living room, he noticed that the faded roses Louise had brought in from the garden smelled more of earth than of anything else. It was a putrid, compelling smell. He dropped the roses into a wastebasket, but not before they had reminded him of the spoiled meat, the whore, and the spider web.

He had started going to parties again, but without the hurdle race to run, the parties of his friends and neighbors seemed to him interminable and stale. He listened to their dirty jokes with an irritability that was hard for him to conceal. Even their countenances discouraged him, and, slumped in a chair, he would regard their skin and their teeth narrowly, as if he were himself a much younger man.

The brunt of his irritability fell on Louise, and it seemed to her that Cash, in losing the hurdle race, had lost the thing that had preserved his equilibrium. He was rude to his friends when they stopped in for a drink. He was rude and gloomy when he and Louise went out. When Louise asked him what was the matter, he only murmured, "Nothing, nothing, nothing," and poured himself some bourbon. May and June passed, and then the first part of July, without his showing any improvement.

Then it is a summer night, a wonderful summer night. The passengers on the eight-fifteen see Shady Hill—if they notice it at all—in a bath of placid golden light. The noise of the train is muffled in the heavy foliage, and the long car windows look like a string of lighted aquarium tanks before they flicker out of sight. Up on the hill, the ladies say to one another, "Smell the grass! Smell the trees!" The Farquarsons are giving another party, and Harry has hung a sign, WHISKEY GULCH, from the rose arbor, and is wearing a chef's white hat and an apron. His guests are still drinking, and the smoke from his meat fire rises, on this windless evening, straight up into the trees.

In the clubhouse on the hill, the first of the formal dances for the young people begins around nine. On Alewives Lane sprinklers continue to play after dark. You can smell the water. The air seems as fragrant as it is dark—it is a delicious element to walk through—and most of the windows on Alewives Lane are open to it. You can see Mr. and Mrs. Bearden, as you pass, looking at their television. Joe Lockwood, the young lawyer who lives on the corner, is practicing a speech to the jury before his wife. "I intend to show you," he says, "that a man of probity, a man whose reputation for honesty and reliability . . ." He waves his bare arms as he speaks. His wife goes on knitting. Mrs. Carver—Harry Farquarson's mother-in-law—glances up at the sky and asks, "*Where* did all the stars come from?" She is old and foolish, and yet she is right: Last night's stars seem to have drawn to themselves a new range of galaxies, and the night sky is not dark at all, except where there is a tear in the membrane of light. In the unsold house lots near the track a hermit thrush is singing.

The Bentleys are at home. Poor Cash has been so rude and gloomy that the Farquarsons have not asked him to their party. He sits on the sofa beside Louise, who is sewing elastic into the children's underpants. Through the open window he can hear the pleasant sounds of the summer night. There is another party, in the Rogerses' garden, behind the Bentleys'. The music from the dance drifts down the hill. The band is sketchy—saxophone, drums, and piano—and all the selections are twenty years old. The band plays "Valencia," and Cash looks tenderly toward Louise, but Louise, tonight, is a discouraging figure. The lamp picks out the gray in her hair. Her apron is stained. Her face seems colorless and drawn. Suddenly, Cash begins frenziedly to beat his feet in time to the music. He sings some gibberish—Jabajabajabajaba—to the distant saxophone. He sighs and goes into the kitchen.

Here a faint, stale smell of cooking clings to the dark. From the kitchen window Cash can see the lights and figures of the Rogerses' party. It is a young people's party. The Rogers girl has asked some friends in for dinner before the dance, and now they seem to be leaving. Cars are driving away. "I'm covered with grass stains," a girl says. "I hope the old man remembered to buy gasoline," a boy says, and a girl laughs. There is nothing on their minds but the passing summer night. Taxes and the elastic in underpants—all the unbeautiful facts of life that threaten to crush the breath out of Cash—have not touched a single figure in this garden. Then jealousy seizes him—such savage and bitter jealousy that he feels ill.

He does not understand what separates him from these children in the garden next door. He has been a young man. He has been a hero. He has been adored and happy and full of animal spirits, and now he stands in a dark kitchen, deprived of his athletic prowess, his impetuousness, his good looks—of everything that means anything to him. He feels as if the figures in the next yard are the specters from some party in that past where all his tastes and desires lie, and from which he has been cruelly removed. He feels like a ghost of the summer evening. He is sick with longing. Then he hears voices in the front of the house. Louise turns on the kitchen light. "Oh, here you are," she says. "The Beardens stopped in. I think they'd like a drink."

Cash went to the front of the house to greet the Beardens. They wanted to go up to the club, for one dance. They saw, at a glance, that Cash was at loose ends, and they urged the Bentleys to come. Louise got someone to stay with the children and then went upstairs to change.

When they got to the club, they found a few friends of their age hanging around the bar, but Cash did not stay in the bar. He seemed restless and perhaps drunk. He banged into a table on his way through the lounge to the ballroom. He cut in on a young girl. He seized her too vehemently and jigged her off in an ancient two-step. She signaled openly for help to a boy in the stag line, and Cash was cut out. He walked angrily off the dance floor onto the terrace. Some young couples there withdrew from one another's arms as he pushed open the screen door. He walked to the end of the terrace, where he hoped to be alone, but here he surprised another young couple, who got up from the lawn, where they seemed to have been lying, and walked off in the dark toward the pool.

Louise remained in the bar with the Beardens. "Poor Cash is tight," she said. And then, "He told me this afternoon that he was going to paint the storm windows," she said. "Well, he mixed the paint and washed the brushes and put on some old fatigues and went into the cellar. There was a telephone call for him at around five, and when I went down to tell him, do you know what he was doing? He was just sitting there in the dark with a cocktail shaker. He hadn't touched the storm windows. He was just sitting there in the dark, drinking Martinis."

"Poor Cash," Trace said.

"You ought to get a job," Lucy said. "That would give you emotional and financial independence." As she spoke, they all heard the noise of furniture being moved around in the lounge.

"Oh, my God!" Louise said. "He's going to run the race. Stop him, Trace, stop him! He'll hurt himself. He'll kill himself!"

They all went to the door of the lounge. Louise again asked

Trace to interfere, but she could see by Cash's face that he was way beyond remonstrating with. A few couples left the dance floor and stood watching the preparations. Trace didn't try to stop Cash—he helped him. There was no pistol, so he slammed a couple of books together for the start.

Over the sofa went Cash, over the coffee table, the lamp table, the fire screen, and the hassock. All his grace and strength seemed to have returned to him. He cleared the big sofa at the end of the room and instead of stopping there, he turned and started back over the course. His face was strained. His mouth hung open. The tendons of his neck protruded hideously. He made the hassock, the fire screen, the lamp table, and the coffee table. People held their breath when he approached the final sofa, but he cleared it and landed on his feet. There was some applause. Then he groaned and fell. Louise ran to his side. His clothes were soaked with sweat and he gasped for breath. She knelt down beside him and took his head in her lap and stroked his thin hair.

Cash had a terrible hangover on Sunday, and Louise let him sleep until it was nearly time for church. The family went off to Christ Church together at eleven, as they always did. Cash sang, prayed, and got to his knees, but the most he ever felt in church was that he stood outside the realm of God's infinite mercy, and, to tell the truth, he no more believed in the Father, the Son, and the Holy Ghost than does my bull terrier. They returned home at one to eat the overcooked meat and stony potatoes that were their customary Sunday lunch. At around five, the Parminters called up and asked them over for a drink. Louise didn't want to go, so Cash went alone. (Oh, those suburban Sunday nights, those Sunday-night blues! Those departing weekend guests, those stale cocktails, those half-dead flowers, those trips to Harmon to catch the Century, those post-mortems and pickup suppers!) It was sultry and overcast. The dog days were beginning. He drank gin with the Parminters for an hour or two and then went over to the Townsends' for a drink. The Farquarsons called up the Townsends and asked them to come over and bring Cash with them, and at the Farquarsons' they had some more drinks and ate the leftover party food. The Farquarsons were glad to see that Cash seemed like himself again. It was half past ten or eleven when he got home. Louise was upstairs, cutting out of the current copy of *Life* those scenes of mayhem, disaster, and violent death that she felt might corrupt her children. She always did this. Cash came upstairs and spoke to her and then went down again. In a little while, she heard him moving the living-room furniture around. Then he called to her, and when she went down, he was standing at the foot of the stairs in his stocking feet, holding the pistol out to her. She had never fired it before, and the directions he gave her were not much help.

"Hurry up," he said. "I can't wait all night."

He had forgotten to tell her about the safety, and when she pulled the trigger nothing happened.

"It's that little lever," he said. "Press that little lever." Then, in his impatience, he hurdled the sofa anyhow.

The pistol went off and Louise got him in midair. She shot him dead.

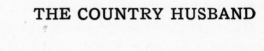

THE COUNTRY HUSBAND

✳ **TO BEGIN** at the beginning, the airplane from Minneapolis in which Francis Weed was traveling East ran into heavy weather. The sky had been a hazy blue, with the clouds below the plane lying so close together that nothing could be seen of the earth. Then mist began to form outside the windows, and they flew into a white cloud of such density that it reflected the exhaust fires. The color of the cloud darkened to gray, and the plane began to rock. Francis had been in heavy weather before, but he had never been shaken up so much. The man in the seat beside him pulled a flask out of his pocket and took a drink. Francis smiled at his neighbor, but the man looked away; he wasn't sharing his painkiller with anyone. The plane had begun to drop and flounder wildly. A child was crying. The air in the cabin was overheated and stale, and Francis' left foot went to sleep. He read a little from a paper book that he had bought at the airport, but the violence of the storm divided his attention. It was black outside the ports. The exhaust fires blazed and shed sparks in the dark, and, inside, the shaded lights, the stuffiness, and the window curtains gave the cabin an atmosphere of intense and misplaced domesticity. Then the lights flickered and went out. "You know what I've always wanted to do?" the man beside Francis said suddenly. "I've always wanted to buy a farm in New Hampshire and raise beef cattle." The stewardess announced that they were going to make an emergency landing. All but the child saw in their minds the spreading wings of the Angel of Death. The pilot could be heard singing faintly, "I've got sixpence, jolly, jolly sixpence. I've got sixpence to last me all my life . . ." There was no other sound.

The loud groaning of the hydraulic valves swallowed up the pilot's song, and there was a shrieking high in the air, like automobile brakes, and the plane hit flat on its belly in a cornfield and shook them so violently that an old man up forward howled, "Me kidneys! Me kidneys!" The stewardess flung open the door, and someone opened an emergency door at the back, letting in the sweet noise of their continuing mortality—the idle splash and smell of a heavy rain. Anxious for their lives, they filed out of the doors and scattered over the cornfield in all directions, praying that the thread would hold. It did. Nothing happened. When it was clear that the plane would not burn or explode, the crew and the stewardess gathered the passengers together and led them to the shelter of a barn. They were not far from Philadelphia, and in a little while a string of taxis took them into the city. "It's just like the Marne," someone said, but there was surprisingly little relaxation of that suspiciousness with which many Americans regard their fellow-travelers.

In Philadelphia, Francis Weed got a train to New York. At the end of that journey, he crossed the city and caught, just as it was about to pull out, the commuting train that he took five nights a week to his home in Shady Hill.

He sat with Trace Bearden. "You know, I was in that plane that just crashed outside Philadelphia," he said. "We came down in a field . . ." He had traveled faster than the newspapers or the rain, and the weather in New York was sunny and mild. It was a day in late September, as fragrant and shapely as an apple. Trace listened to the story, but how could he get excited? Francis had no powers that would let him re-create a brush with death—particularly in the atmosphere of a commuting train, journeying through a sunny countryside where already, in the slum gardens, there were signs of harvest. Trace picked up his newspaper, and Francis was left alone with his thoughts. He said good night to Trace on the platform at Shady Hill and drove in his secondhand Volkswagen up to the Blenhollow neighborhood, where he lived.

The Weeds' Dutch Colonial house was larger than it appeared to be from the driveway. The living room was spacious and divided like Gaul into three parts. Around an ell to the left as one entered from the vestibule was the long table, laid for six, with candles and a bowl of fruit in the center. The sounds and smells that came from the open kitchen door were appetizing, for Julia Weed was a good cook. The largest part of the living room centered around a fireplace. On the right were some bookshelves and a piano. The room was polished and tranquil, and from the windows that opened to the west there was some late-summer sunlight, brilliant and as clear as water. Nothing here was neglected;

nothing had not been burnished. It was not the kind of household where, after prying open a stuck cigarette box, you would find an old shirt button and a tarnished nickel. The hearth was swept, the roses on the piano were reflected in the polish of the broad top, and there was an album of Schubert waltzes on the rack. Louisa Weed, a pretty girl of nine, was looking out the western windows. Her younger brother Henry was standing beside her. Her still younger brother, Toby, was studying the figures of some tonsured monks drinking beer on the polished brass of the wood box. Francis, taking off his hat and putting down his paper, was not consciously pleased with the scene; he was not that reflective. It was his element, his creation, and he returned to it with that sense of lightness and strength with which any creature returns to its home. "Hi, everybody," he said. "The plane from Minneapolis . . ."

Nine times out of ten, Francis would be greeted with affection, but tonight the children are absorbed in their own antagonisms. Francis has not finished his sentence about the plane crash before Henry plants a kick in Louisa's behind. Louisa swings around, saying, "*Damn* you!" Francis makes the mistake of scolding Louisa for bad language before he punishes Henry. Now Louisa turns on her father and accuses him of favoritism. Henry is always right; she is persecuted and lonely; her lot is hopeless. Francis turns to his son, but the boy has justification for the kick—she hit him first; she hit him on the ear, which is dangerous. Louisa agrees with this passionately. She hit him on the ear, and she *meant* to hit him on the ear, because he messed up her china collection. Henry says that this is a lie. Little Toby turns away from

52

the wood box to throw in some evidence for Louisa. Henry claps his hand over little Toby's mouth. Francis separates the two boys but accidentally pushes Toby into the wood box. Toby begins to cry. Louisa is already crying. Just then, Julia Weed comes into that part of the room where the table is laid. She is a pretty, intelligent woman, and the white in her hair is premature. She does not seem to notice the fracas. "Hello, darling," she says serenely to Francis. "Wash your hands, everyone. Dinner is ready." She strikes a match and lights the six candles in this vale of tears.

This simple announcement, like the war cries of the Scottish chieftains, only refreshes the ferocity of the combatants. Louisa gives Henry a blow on the shoulder. Henry, although he seldom cries, has pitched nine innings and is tired. He bursts into tears. Little Toby discovers a splinter in his hand and begins to howl. Francis says loudly that he has been in a plane crash and that he is tired. Julia appears again, from the kitchen, and, still ignoring the chaos, asks Francis to go upstairs and tell Helen that everything is ready. Francis is happy to go; it is like getting back to headquarters company. He is planning to tell his oldest daughter about the airplane crash, but Helen is lying on her bed reading a *True Romance* magazine, and the first thing Francis does is to take the magazine from her hand and remind Helen that he has forbidden her to buy it. She did not buy it, Helen replies. It was given to her by her best friend, Bessie Black. Everybody reads *True Romance*. Bessie Black's father reads *True Romance*. There isn't a girl in Helen's class who doesn't read *True Romance*. Francis expresses his detestation of the magazine and then tells her that dinner is ready—although

53

from the sounds downstairs it doesn't seem so. Helen follows him down the stairs. Julia has seated herself in the candle-light and spread a napkin over her lap. Neither Louisa nor Henry has come to the table. Little Toby is still howling, lying face down on the floor. Francis speaks to him gently: "Daddy was in a plane crash this afternoon, Toby. Don't you want to hear about it?" Toby goes on crying. "If you don't come to the table now. Toby," Francis says, "I'll have to send you to bed without any supper." The little boy rises, gives him a cutting look, flies up the stairs to his bedroom, and slams the door. "Oh dear," Julia says, and starts to go after him. Francis says that she will spoil him. Julia says that Toby is ten pounds underweight and has to be encouraged to eat. Winter is coming, and he will spend the cold months in bed unless he has his dinner. Julia goes upstairs. Francis sits down at the table with Helen. Helen is suffering from the dismal feeling of having read too intently on a fine day, and she gives her father and the room a jaded look. She doesn't understand about the plane crash, because there wasn't a drop of rain in Shady Hill.

Julia returns with Toby, and they all sit down and are served. "Do I have to look at that big, fat slob?" Henry says, of Louisa. Everybody but Toby enters into this skirmish, and it rages up and down the table for five minutes. Toward the end, Henry puts his napkin over his head and, trying to eat that way, spills spinach all over his shirt. Francis asks Julia if the children couldn't have their dinner earlier. Julia's guns are loaded for this. She can't cook two dinners and lay two tables. She paints with lightning strokes that panorama of drudgery in which her youth, her beauty, and her wit have been lost. Francis says that he must be understood; he was nearly killed in an airplane crash, and he doesn't like to come home every night to a battlefield. Now Julia is deeply committed. Her voice trembles. He doesn't come home every night to a battlefield. The accusation is stupid and mean. Everything was tranquil until he arrived. She stops speaking, puts down her knife and fork, and looks into her plate as if it is a gulf. She begins to cry. "Poor Mummy!" Toby says, and when Julia gets up from the table, drying her tears with a napkin, Toby goes to her side. "Poor Mummy," he says. "Poor Mummy!" And they climb the stairs together. The other children drift away from the battlefield, and Francis goes into the back garden for a cigarette and some air.

It was a pleasant garden, with walks and flower beds and places to sit. The sunset had nearly burned out, but there was still plenty of light. Put into a thoughtful mood by the crash and the battle, Francis listened to the evening sounds of Shady Hill. "Varmints! Rascals!" old Mr. Nixon shouted to the squirrels in his bird-feeding station. "Avaunt and quit my sight!" A door slammed. Someone was playing tennis on the Babcocks' court; someone was cutting grass. Then Donald Goslin, who lived at the corner, began to play the "Moonlight Sonata." He did this nearly every night. He threw the tempo out the window and played it *rubato* from beginning to end, like an outpouring of tearful petulance, lonesomeness, and self-pity—of everything it was Beethoven's greatness not to know. The music rang up and down the street beneath the trees like an appeal for love, for tenderness, aimed at some lonely housemaid—some fresh-faced, homesick girl from Galway, looking at old snapshots in her third-floor room. "Here, Jupiter, here, Jupiter," Francis called to the Mercers' retriever. Jupiter crashed through the tomato vines with the remains of a felt hat in his mouth.

Jupiter was an anomaly. His retrieving instincts and his high spirits were out of place in Shady Hill. He was as black as coal, with a long, alert, intelligent, rakehell face. His eyes gleamed with mischief, and he held his head high. It was the fierce, heavily collared dog's head that appears in heraldry, in tapestry, and that used to appear on umbrella handles and walking sticks. Jupiter went where he pleased, ransacking wastebaskets, clotheslines, garbage pails, and shoe bags. He broke up garden parties and tennis matches, and got mixed up in the processional at Christ Church on Sunday, barking at the men in red dresses. He crashed through old Mr. Nixon's rose garden two or three times a day, cutting a wide swath through the Condesa de Sastagos, and as soon as Donald Goslin lighted his barbecue fire on Thursday nights, Jupiter would get the scent. Nothing the Goslins did could drive him away. Sticks and stones and rude commands only moved him to the edge of the terrace, where he remained, with his gallant and heraldic muzzle, waiting for Donald Goslin to turn his back and reach for the salt. Then he would spring onto the terrace, lift the steak lightly off the fire, and run away with the Goslins' dinner. Jupiter's days were numbered. The Wrightsons' German gardener or the Farquarsons' cook would soon poison him. Even old Mr. Nixon might put some arsenic in the garbage that Jupiter loved. "Here, Jupiter, Jupiter!" Francis called, but the dog pranced off, shaking the hat in his white teeth. Looking in

at the windows of his house, Francis saw that Julia had come
down and was blowing out the candles.

Julia and Francis Weed went out a great deal. Julia was
well liked and gregarious, and her love of parties sprang
from a most natural dread of chaos and loneliness. She went
through her morning mail with real anxiety, looking for invitations, and she usually found some, but she was insatiable,
and if she had gone out seven nights a week, it would not
have cured her of a reflective look—the look of someone who
hears distant music—for she would always suppose that
there was a more brilliant party somewhere else. Francis
limited her to two week-night parties, putting a flexible inter-
pretation on Friday, and rode through the weekend like a
dory in a gale. The day after the airplane crash, the Weeds
were to have dinner with the Farquarsons.

Francis got home late from town, and Julia got the sitter
while he dressed, and then hurried him out of the house. The
party was small and pleasant, and Francis settled down to
enjoy himself. A new maid passed the drinks. Her hair was
dark, and her face was round and pale and seemed familiar
to Francis. He had not developed his memory as a sentimental faculty. Wood smoke, lilac, and other such perfumes
did not stir him, and his memory was something like his
appendix—a vestigial repository. It was not his limitation at
all to be unable to escape the past; it was perhaps his limitation that he had escaped it so successfully. He might have
seen the maid at other parties, he might have seen her taking
a walk on Sunday afternoons, but in either case he would not
be searching his memory now. Her face was, in a wonderful

way, a moon face—Norman or Irish—but it was not beautiful enough to account for his feeling that he had seen her before, in circumstances that he ought to be able to remember. He asked Nellie Farquarson who she was. Nellie said that the maid had come through an agency, and that her home was Trénon, in Normandy—a small place with a church and a restaurant that Nellie had once visited. While Nellie talked on about her travels abroad, Francis realized where he had seen the woman before. It had been at the end of the war. He had left a replacement depot with some other men and taken a three-day pass in Trénon. On their second day, they had walked out to a crossroads to see the public chastisement of a young woman who had lived with the German commandant during the Occupation.

It was a cool morning in the fall. The sky was overcast, and poured down onto the dirt crossroads a very discouraging light. They were on high land and could see how like one another the shapes of the clouds and the hills were as they stretched off toward the sea. The prisoner arrived sitting on a three-legged stool in a farm cart. She stood by the cart while the mayor read the accusation and the sentence. Her head was bent and her face was set in that empty half smile behind which the whipped soul is suspended. When the mayor was finished, she undid her hair and let it fall across her back. A little man with a gray mustache cut off her hair with shears and dropped it on the ground. Then, with a bowl of soapy water and a straight razor, he shaved her skull clean. A woman approached and began to undo the fastenings of her clothes, but the prisoner pushed her aside and undressed herself. When she pulled her chemise over her head and threw it on the ground, she was naked. The women jeered; the men were still. There was no change in the falseness or the plaintiveness of the prisoner's smile. The cold wind made her white skin rough and hardened the nipples of her breasts. The jeering ended gradually, put down by the recognition of their common humanity. One woman spat on her, but some inviolable grandeur in her nakedness lasted through the ordeal. When the crowd was quiet, she turned —she had begun to cry—and, with nothing on but a pair of worn black shoes and stockings, walked down the dirt road alone away from the village. The round white face had aged a little, but there was no question but that the maid who passed his cocktails and later served Francis his dinner was the woman who had been punished at the crossroads.

The war seemed now so distant and that world where the cost of partisanship had been death or torture so long ago. Francis had lost track of the men who had been with him in Vésey. He could not count on Julia's discretion. He could not tell anyone. And if he had told the story now, at the dinner table, it would have been a social as well as a human error. The people in the Farquarsons' living room seemed united in their tacit claim that there had been no past, no war—that there was no danger or trouble in the world. In the recorded history of human arrangements, this extraordinary meeting would have fallen into place, but the atmosphere of Shady Hill made the memory unseemly and impolite. The prisoner withdrew after passing the coffee, but the encounter left Francis feeling languid; it had opened his memory and his senses, and left them dilated. He and Julia drove home when the party ended, and Julia went into the house. Francis stayed in the car to take the sitter home.

Expecting to see Mrs. Henlein, the old lady who usually stayed with the children, he was surprised when a young girl opened the door and came out onto the lighted stoop. She stayed in the light to count her textbooks. She was frowning and beautiful. Now, the world is full of beautiful young girls, but Francis saw here the difference between beauty and perfection. All those endearing flaws, moles, birthmarks, and healed wounds were missing, and he experienced in his consciousness that moment when music breaks glass, and felt a pang of recognition as strange, deep, and wonderful as anything in his life. It hung from her frown, from an impalpable darkness in her face—a look that impressed him as a direct appeal for love. When she had counted her books, she came down the steps and opened the car door. In the light, he saw that her cheeks were wet. She got in and shut the door.

"You're new," Francis said.

"Yes. Mrs. Henlein is sick. I'm Anne Murchison."

"Did the children give you any trouble?"

"Oh, no, no." She turned and smiled at him unhappily in the dim dashboard light. Her light hair caught on the collar of her jacket, and she shook her head to set it loose.

"You've been crying."

"Yes."

"I hope it was nothing that happened in our house."

"No, no, it was nothing that happened in your house." Her voice was bleak. "It's no secret. Everybody in the village knows. Daddy's an alcoholic, and he just called me from some saloon and gave me a piece of his mind. He thinks I'm im-

60

moral. He called just before Mrs. Weed came back."

"I'm sorry."

"Oh, *Lord!*" She gasped and began to cry. She turned toward Francis, and he took her in his arms and let her cry on his shoulder. She shook in his embrace, and this movement accentuated his sense of the fineness of her flesh and bone. The layers of their clothing felt thin, and when her shuddering began to diminish, it was so much like a paroxysm of love that Francis lost his head and pulled her roughly against him. She drew away. "I live on Belleview Avenue," she said. "You go down Lansing Street to the railroad bridge."

"All right." He started the car.

"You turn left at that traffic light. . . . Now you turn right here and go straight on toward the tracks."

The road Francis took brought him out of his own neighborhood, across the tracks, and toward the river, to a street where the near-poor lived, in houses whose peaked gables and trimmings of wooden lace conveyed the purest feelings of pride and romance, although the houses themselves could not have offered much privacy or comfort, they were all so small. The street was dark, and, stirred by the grace and beauty of the troubled girl, he seemed, in turning in to it, to have come into the deepest part of some submerged memory. In the distance, he saw a porch light burning. It was the only one, and she said that the house with the light was where she lived. When he stopped the car, he could see beyond the porch light into a dimly lighted hallway with an old-fashioned clothes tree. "Well, here we are," he said, conscious that a young man would have said something different.

She did not move her hands from the books, where they

were folded, and she turned and faced him. There were tears of lust in his eyes. Determinedly—not sadly—he opened the door on his side and walked around to open hers. He took her free hand, letting his fingers in between hers, climbed at her side the two concrete steps, and went up a narrow walk through a front garden where dahlias, marigolds, and roses —things that had withstood the light frosts—still bloomed, and made a bittersweet smell in the night air. At the steps, she freed her hand and then turned and kissed him swiftly. Then she crossed the porch and shut the door. The porch light went out, then the light in the hall. A second later, a light went on upstairs at the side of the house, shining into a tree that was still covered with leaves. It took her only a few minutes to undress and get into bed, and then the house was dark.

Julia was asleep when Francis got home. He opened a second window and got into bed to shut his eyes on that night, but as soon as they were shut—as soon as he had dropped off to sleep—the girl entered his mind, moving with perfect freedom through its shut doors and filling chamber after chamber with her light, her perfume, and the music of her voice. He was crossing the Atlantic with her on the old *Mauretania* and, later, living with her in Paris. When he woke from his dream, he got up and smoked a cigarette at the open window. Getting back into bed, he cast around in his mind for something he desired to do that would injure no one, and he thought of skiing. Up through the dimness in his mind rose the image of a mountain deep in snow. It was late in the day. Wherever his eyes looked, he saw broad and heartening things. Over his shoulder, their was a snow-filled valley, rising into wooded hills where the trees dimmed the whiteness like a sparse coat of hair. The cold deadened all sound but the loud, iron clanking of the lift machinery. The light on the trails was blue, and it was harder than it had been a minute or two earlier to pick the turns, harder to judge—now that the snow was all deep blue—the crust, the ice, the bare spots, and the deep piles of dry powder. Down the mountain he swung, matching his speed against the contours of a slope that had been formed in the first ice age, seeking with ardor some simplicity of feeling and circumstance. Night fell then, and he drank a Martini with some old friend in a dirty country bar.

In the morning, Francis' snow-covered mountain was gone, and he was left with his vivid memories of Paris and the *Mauretania*. He had been bitten gravely. He washed his body, shaved his jaws, drank his coffee, and missed the seventhirty-one. The train pulled out just as he brought his car to the station, and the longing he felt for the coaches as they drew stubbornly away from him reminded him of the humors of love. He waited for the eight-two, on what was now an empty platform. It was a clear morning; the morning seemed thrown like a gleaming bridge of light over his mixed affairs. His spirits were feverish and high. The image of the girl seemed to put him into a relationship to the world that was mysterious and enthralling. Cars were beginning to fill up the parking lot, and he noticed that those that had driven down from the high land above Shady Hill were white with hoarfrost. This first clear sign of autumn thrilled him. An express train—a night train from Buffalo or Albany—came down the tracks between the platforms, and he saw that the roofs of the foremost cars were covered with a skin of ice. Struck by the miraculous physicalness of everything, he smiled at the passengers in the dining car, who could be seen eating eggs and wiping their mouths with napkins as they traveled. The sleeping-car compartments, with their soiled bed linen, trailed through the fresh morning like a string of rooming-house windows. Then he saw an extraordinary thing; at one of the bedroom windows sat an unclothed woman of exceptional beauty, combing her golden hair. She passed like an apparition through Shady Hill, combing and combing her hair, and Francis followed her with his eyes until she was out of sight. Then old Mrs. Wrightson joined him on the platform and began to talk.

"Well, I guess you must be surprised to see me here the third morning in a row," she said, "but because of my window curtains I'm becoming a regular commuter. The curtains I bought on Monday I returned on Tuesday, and the curtains I bought Tuesday I'm returning today. On Monday, I got exactly what I wanted—it's a wool tapestry with roses and birds—but when I got them home, I found they were the wrong length. Well, I exchanged them yesterday, and when I got them home, I found they were still the wrong length. Now I'm praying to high Heaven that the decorator will have them in the right length, because you know my house, you *know* my living-room windows, and you can imagine what a problem they present. I don't know what to do with them."

"I know what to do with them," Francis said.

"What?"

"Paint them black on the inside, and shut up."

There was a gasp from Mrs. Wrightson, and Francis

looked down at her to be sure that she knew he meant to be rude. She turned and walked away from him, so damaged in spirit that she limped. A wonderful feeling enveloped him, as if light were being shaken about him, and he thought again of Venus combing and combing her hair as she drifted through the Bronx. The realization of how many years had passed since he had enjoyed being deliberately impolite sobered him. Among his friends and neighbors, there were brilliant and gifted people—he saw that—but many of them, also, were bores and fools, and he had made the mistake of listening to them all with equal attention. He had confused a lack of discrimination with Christian love, and the confusion semed general and destructive. He was grateful to the girl for this bracing sensation of independence. Birds were singing—cardinals and the last of the robins. The sky shone like enamel. Even the smell of ink from his morning paper honed his appetite for life, and the world that was spread out around him was plainly a paradise.

If Francis had believed in some hierarchy of love—in spirits armed with hunting bows, in the capriciousness of Venus and Eros—or even in magical potions, philters, and stews, in scapulae and quarters of the moon, it might have explained his susceptibility and his feverish high spirits. The autumnal loves of middle age are well publicized, and he guessed that he was face to face with one of these, but there was not a trace of autumn in what he felt. He wanted to sport in the green woods, scratch where he itched, and drink from the same cup.

His secretary, Miss Rainey, was late that morning—she went to a psychiatrist three mornings a week—and when she came in, Francis wondered what advice a psychiatrist would have for him. But the girl promised to bring back into his life something like the sound of music. The realization that this music might lead him straight to a trial for statutory rape at the county courthouse collapsed his happiness. The photograph of his four children laughing into the camera on the beach at Gay Head reproached him. On the letterhead of his firm there was a drawing of the Laocoön, and the figure of the priest and his sons in the coils of the snake appeared to him to have the deepest meaning.

He had lunch with Pinky Trabert. At a conversational level, the mores of his friends were robust and elastic, but he knew that the moral card house would come down on them all—on Julia and the children as well—if he got caught taking advantage of a babysitter. Looking back over the recent history of Shady Hill for some precedent, he found there was none. There was no turpitude; there had not been a divorce since he lived there; there had not even been a breath of scandal. Things seemed arranged with more propriety even than in the Kingdom of Heaven. After leaving Pinky, Francis went to a jeweler's and bought the girl a bracelet. How happy this clandestine purchase made him, how stuffy and comical the jeweler's clerks seemed, how sweet the women who passed at his back smelled! On Fifth Avenue, passing Atlas with his shoulders bent under the weight of the world, Francis thought of the strenuousness of containing his physicalness within the patterns he had chosen.

He did not know when he would see the girl next. He had the bracelet in his inside pocket when he got home. Opening the door of his house, he found her in the hall.

Her back was to him, and she turned when she heard the door close. Her smile was open and loving. Her perfection stunned him like a fine day—a day after a thunderstorm. He seized her and covered her lips with his, and she struggled but she did not have to struggle for long, because just then little Gertrude Flannery appeared from somewhere and said, "Oh, Mr. Weed . . ."

Gertrude was a stray. She had been born with a taste for exploration, and she did not have it in her to center her life with her affectionate parents. People who did not know the Flannerys concluded from Gertrude's behavior that she was the child of a bitterly divided family, where drunken quarrels were the rule. This was not true. The fact that little Gertrude's clothing was ragged and thin was her own triumph over her mother's struggle to dress her warmly and neatly. Garrulous, skinny, and unwashed, she drifted from house to house around the Blenhollow neighborhood, forming and breaking alliances based on an attachment to babies, animals, children her own age, adolescents, and sometimes adults. Opening your front door in the morning, you would find Gertrude sitting on your stoop. Going into the bathroom to shave, you would find Gertrude using the toilet. Looking into your son's crib, you would find it empty, and, looking further, you would find that Gertrude had pushed him in his baby carriage into the next village. She was helpful, pervasive, honest, hungry, and loyal. She never went home of her own choice. When the time to go arrived, she was indifferent to all its signs. "Go home, Gertrude," people could be heard saying in one house or another, night after night. "Go home, Gertrude. It's time for you to go home now, Gertrude." "You had better go home and get your supper, Gertrude." "I told you to go home twenty minutes ago, Gertrude." "Your mother will be worrying about you, Gertrude." "Go home, Gertrude, go home."

There are times when the lines around the human eye seem like shelves of eroded stone and when the staring eye itself strikes us with such a wilderness of animal feeling that we are at a loss. The look Francis gave the little girl was ugly and queer, and it frightened her. He reached into his pocket—his hands were shaking—and took out a quarter. "Go home, Gertrude, go home, and don't tell anyone, Gertrude. Don't—" He choked and ran into the living room as Julia called down to him from upstairs to hurry and dress.

The thought that he would drive Anne Murchison home later that night ran like a golden thread through the events of the party that Francis and Julia went to, and he laughed uproariously at dull jokes, dried a tear when Mabel Mercer told him about the death of her kitten, and stretched, yawned, sighed, and grunted like any other man with a rendezvous at the back of his mind. The bracelet was in his pocket. As he sat talking, the smell of grass was in his nose, and he was wondering where he would park the car. Nobody lived in the old Parker mansion, and the driveway was used as a lovers' lane. Townsend Street was a dead end, and he could park there, beyond the last house. The old lane that used to connect Elm Street to the riverbanks was overgrown, but he had walked there with his children, and he could drive his car deep enough into the brushwoods to be concealed.

The Weeds were the last to leave the party, and their host and hostess spoke of their own married happiness while they all four stood in the hallway saying good night. "She's my girl," their host said, squeezing his wife. "She's my blue sky. After sixteen years, I still bite her shoulders. She makes me feel like Hannibal crossing the Alps."

The Weeds drove home in silence. Francis brought the car up the driveway and sat still, with the motor running. "You can put the car in the garage," Julia said as she got out. "I told the Murchison girl she could leave at eleven. Someone drove her home." She shut the door, and Francis sat in the dark. He would be spared nothing then, it seemed, that a fool was not spared: ravening lewdness, jealousy, this hurt to his feelings that put tears in his eyes, even scorn—for he could see clearly the image he now presented, his arms spread over the steering wheel and his head buried in them for love.

Francis had been a dedicated Boy Scout when he was young, and, remembering the precepts of his youth, he left his office early the next afternoon and played some round-robin squash, but, with his body toned up by exercise and a shower, he realized that he might better have stayed at his desk. It was a frosty night when he got home. The air smelled sharply of change. When he stepped into the house, he sensed an unusual stir. The children were in their best clothes, and when Julia came down, she was wearing a lavender dress and her diamond sunburst. She explained the stir: Mr. Hubber was coming at seven to take their photograph for the Christmas card. She had put out Francis' blue suit and a tie with some color in it, because the picture was going to be in color this year. Julia was lighthearted at the thought of being photographed for Christmas. It was the kind of ceremony she enjoyed.

Francis went upstairs to change his clothes. He was tired from the day's work and tired with longing, and sitting on the edge of the bed had the effect of deepening his weariness. He thought of Anne Murchison, and the physical need to express himself, instead of being restrained by the pink lamps on Julia's dressing table, engulfed him. He went to Julia's desk, took a piece of writing paper, and began to write on it. "Dear Anne, I love you, I love you, I love you . . ." No one would see the letter, and he used no restraint. He used phrases like "heavenly bliss," and "love nest." He salivated, sighed, and trembled. When Julia called him to come down, the abyss between his fantasy and the practical world opened so wide that he felt it affect the muscles of his heart.

Julia and the children were on the stoop, and the photographer and his assistant had set up a double battery of floodlights to show the family and the architectural beauty of the entrance to their house. People who had come home on a late train slowed their cars to see the Weeds being photographed for their Christmas card. A few waved and called to the family. It took half an hour of smiling and wetting their lips before Mr. Hubber was satisfied. The heat of the lights made an unfresh smell in the frosty air, and when they were turned off, they lingered on the retina of Francis' eyes.

Later that night, while Francis and Julia were drinking their coffee in the living room, the doorbell rang. Julia answered the door and let in Clayton Thomas. He had come to pay her for some theater tickets that she had given his mother some time ago, and that Helen Thomas had scrupulously insisted on paying for, though Julia had asked her not to. Julia invited him in to have a cup of coffee. "I won't have

any coffee," Clayton said, "but I will come in for a minute."
He followed her into the living room, said good evening
to Francis, and sat awkwardly in a chair.

Clayton's father had been killed in the war, and the young
man's fatherlessness surrounded him like an element. This
may have been conspicuous in Shady Hill because the
Thomases were the only family that lacked a piece; all
the other marriages were intact and productive. Clayton was
in his second or third year of college, and he and his mother
lived alone in a large house, which she hoped to sell. Clayton
had once made some trouble. Years ago, he had stolen some
money and run away; he had got to California before they
caught up with him. He was tall and homely, wore horn-
rimmed glasses, and spoke in a deep voice.

"When do you go back to college, Clayton?" Francis asked.

"I'm not going back," Clayton said. "Mother doesn't have
the money, and there's no sense in all this pretense. I'm going
to get a job, and if we sell the house, we'll take an apartment
in New York."

"Won't you miss Shady Hill?" Julia asked.

"No," Clayton said. "I don't like it."

"Why not?" Francis asked.

"Well, there's a lot here I don't approve of," Clayton said
gravely. "Things like the club dances. Last Saturday night, I
looked in toward the end and saw Mr. Granner trying to put
Mrs. Minot into the trophy case. They were both drunk. I
disapprove of so much drinking."

"It was Saturday night," Francis said.

"And all the dovecotes are phony," Clayton said. "And the
way people clutter up their lives. I've thought about it a lot,

71

and what seems to me to be really wrong with Shady Hill is that it doesn't have any future. So much energy is spent in perpetuating the place—in keeping out undesirables, and so forth—that the only idea of the future anyone has is just more and more commuting trains and more parties. I don't think that's healthy. I think people ought to be able to dream big dreams about the future. I think people ought to be able to dream great dreams."

"It's too bad you couldn't continue with college," Julia said.

"I wanted to go to divinity school," Clayton said.

"What's your church?" Francis asked.

"Unitarian, Theosophist, Transcendentalist, Humanist," Clayton said.

"Wasn't Emerson a transcendentalist?" Julia asked.

"I mean the English transcendentalists," Clayton said. "All the American transcendentalists were goops."

"What kind of a job do you expect to get?" Francis asked.

"Well, I'd like to work for a publisher," Clayton said, "but everyone tells me there's nothing doing. But it's the kind of thing I'm interested in. I'm writing a long verse play about good and evil. Uncle Charlie might get me into a bank, and that would be good for me. I need the discipline. I have a long way to go in forming my character. I have some terrible habits. I talk too much. I think I ought to take vows of silence. I ought to try not to speak for a week, and discipline myself. I've thought of making a retreat at one of the Episcopalian monasteries, but I don't like Trinitarianism."

"Do you have any girl friends?" Francis asked.

"I'm engaged to be married," Clayton said. "Of course, I'm not old enough or rich enough to have my engagement observed or respected or anything, but I bought a simulated emerald for Anne Murchison with the money I made cutting lawns this summer. We're going to be married as soon as she finishes school."

Francis recoiled at the mention of the girl's name. Then a dingy light seemed to emanate from his spirit, showing everything—Julia, the boy, the chairs—in their true colorlessness. It was like a bitter turn of the weather.

"We're going to have a large family," Clayton said. "Her father's a terrible rummy, and I've had my hard times, and we want to have lots of children. Oh, she's wonderful, Mr. and Mrs. Weed, and we have so much in common. We like all the same things. We sent out the same Christmas card last year without planning it, and we both have an allergy to tomatoes, and our eyebrows grow together in the middle. Well, good night."

Julia went to the door with him. When she returned, Francis said that Clayton was lazy, irresponsible, affected, and smelly. Julia said that Francis seemed to be getting intolerant; the Thomas boy was young and should be given a chance. Julia had noticed other cases where Francis had been short-tempered. "Mrs. Wrightson has asked everyone in Shady Hill to her anniversary party but us," she said.

"I'm sorry, Julia."

"Do you know why they didn't ask us?"

"Why?"

"Because you insulted Mrs. Wrightson."

"Then you know about it?"

"June Masterson told me. She was standing behind you."

Julia walked in front of the sofa with a small step that

expressed, Francis knew, a feeling of anger.

"I did insult Mrs. Wrightson, Julia, and I meant to. I've never liked her parties, and I'm glad she's dropped us."

"What about Helen?"

"How does Helen come into this?"

"Mrs. Wrightson's the one who decides who goes to the assemblies."

"You mean she can keep Helen from going to the dances?"

"Yes."

"I hadn't thought of that."

"Oh, I knew you hadn't thought of it," Julia cried, thrusting hilt-deep into this chink of his armor. "And it makes me furious to see this kind of stupid thoughtlessness wreck everyone's happiness."

"I don't think I've wrecked anyone's happiness."

"Mrs. Wrightson runs Shady Hill and has run it for the last forty years. I don't know what makes you think that in a community like this you can indulge every impulse you have to be insulting, vulgar, and offensive."

"I have very good manners," Francis said, trying to give the evening a turn toward the light.

"Damn you, Francis Weed!" Julia cried, and the spit of her words struck him in the face. "I've worked hard for the social position we enjoy in this place, and I won't stand by and see you wreck it. You must have understood when you settled here that you couldn't expect to live like a bear in a cave."

"I've got to express my likes and dislikes."

"You can conceal your dislikes. You don't have to meet everything head-on, like a child. Unless you're anxious to be a social leper. It's no accident that we get asked out a great deal. It's no accident that Helen has so many friends. How would you like to spend your Saturday nights at the movies? How would you like to spend your Sundays raking up dead leaves? How would you like it if your daughter spent the assembly nights sitting at her window, listening to the music from the club? How would you like it—" He did something then that was, after all, not so unaccountable, since her words seemed to raise up between them a wall so deadening that he gagged: He struck her full in the face. She staggered and then, a moment later, seemed composed. She went up the stairs to their room. She didn't slam the door. When Francis followed, a few minutes later, he found her packing a suitcase.

"Julia, I'm very sorry."

"It doesn't matter," she said. She was crying.

"Where do you think you're going?"

"I don't know. I just looked at a timetable. There's an eleven-sixteen into New York. I'll take that."

"You can't go, Julia."

"I can't stay. I know that."

"I'm sorry about Mrs. Wrightson, Julia, and I'm—"

"It doesn't matter about Mrs. Wrightson. That isn't the trouble."

"What is the trouble?"

"You don't love me."

"I do love you, Julia."

"No, you don't."

"Julia, I do love you, and I would like to be as we were—sweet and bawdy and dark—but now there are so many people."

75

"You hate me."

"I don't hate you, Julia."

"You have no idea of how much you hate me. I think it's subconscious. You don't realize the cruel things you've done."

"What cruel things, Julia?"

"The cruel acts your subconscious drives you to in order to express your hatred of me."

"What, Julia?"

"I've never complained."

"Tell me."

"You don't know what you're doing."

"Tell me."

"Your clothes."

"What do you mean?"

"I mean the way you leave your dirty clothes around in order to express your subconscious hatred of me."

"I don't understand."

"I mean your dirty socks and your dirty pajamas and your dirty underwear and your dirty shirts!" She rose from kneeling by the suitcase and faced him, her eyes blazing and her voice ringing with emotion. "I'm talking about the fact that you've never learned to hang up anything. You just leave your clothes all over the floor where they drop, in order to humiliate me. You do it on purpose!" She fell on the bed, sobbing.

"Julia, darling!" he said, but when she felt his hand on her shoulder she got up.

"Leave me alone," she said. "I have to go." She brushed past him to the closet and came back with a dress. "I'm not taking any of the things you've given me," she said. "I'm leaving my pearls and the fur jacket."

"Oh, Julia!" Her figure, so helpless in its self-deceptions, bent over the suitcase made him nearly sick with pity. She did not understand how desolate her life would be without him. She didn't understand the hours that working women have to keep. She didn't understand that most of her friendships existed within the framework of their marriage, and that without this she would find herself alone. She didn't understand about travel, about hotels, about money. "Julia, I can't let you go! What you don't understand, Julia, is that you've come to be dependent on me."

She tossed her head back and covered her face with her hands. "Did you say that *I* was dependent on *you*?" she asked. "Is that what you said? And who is it that tells you what time to get up in the morning and when to go to bed at night? Who is it that prepares your meals and picks up your dirty closet and invites your friends to dinner? If it weren't for me, your neckties would be greasy and your clothing would be full of moth holes. You were alone when I met you, Francis Weed, and you'll be alone when I leave. When Mother asked you for a list to send out invitations to our wedding, how many names did you have to give her? Fourteen!"

"Cleveland wasn't my home, Julia."

"And how many of your friends came to the church? Two!"

"Cleveland wasn't my home, Julia."

"Since I'm not taking the fur jacket," she said quietly, "you'd better put it back into storage. There's an insurance policy on the pearls that comes due in January. The name of the laundry and the maid's telephone number—all those things are in my desk. I hope you won't drink too much, Francis. I hope that nothing bad will happen to you. If you do get into serious trouble, you can call me."

"Oh, my darling, I can't let you go!" Francis said. "I can't let you go, Julia!" He took her in his arms.

"I guess I'd better stay and take care of you for a little while longer," she said.

Riding to work in the morning, Francis saw the girl walk down the aisle of the coach. He was surprised; he hadn't realized that the school she went to was in the city, but she was carrying books, she seemed to be going to school. His surprise delayed his reaction, but then he got up clumsily and stepped into the aisle. Several people had come between them, but he could see her ahead of him, waiting for someone to open the car door, and then, as the train swerved, putting out her hand to support herself as she crossed the platform into the next car. He followed her through that car and halfway through another before calling her name— "Anne! Anne!"—but she didn't turn. He followed her into still another car, and she sat down in an aisle seat. Coming up to her, all his feelings warm and bent in her direction, he put his hand on the back of her seat—even this touch warmed him—and, leaning down to speak to her, he saw that it was not Anne. It was an older woman wearing glasses. He went on deliberately into another car, his face red with embarrassment and the much deeper feeling of having his good sense challenged; for if he couldn't tell one person from another, what evidence was there that his life with Julia and the children had as much reality as his dreams of iniquity in Paris or the litter, the grass smell, and the cave-shaped trees in Lovers' Lane.

Late that afternoon, Julia called to remind Francis that

they were going out for dinner. A few minutes later, Trace Bearden called. "Look, fellar," Trace said. "I'm calling for Mrs. Thomas. You know? Clayton, that boy of hers, doesn't seem able to get a job, and I wondered if you could help. If you'd call Charlie Bell—I know he's indebted to you—and say a good word for the kid, I think Charlie would—"

"Trace, I hate to say this," Francis said, "but I don't feel that I can do anything for that boy. The kid's worthless. I know it's a harsh thing to say, but it's a fact. Any kindness done for him would backfire in everybody's face. He's just a worthless kid, Trace, and there's nothing to be done about it. Even if we got him a job, he wouldn't be able to keep it for a week. I know that to be a fact. It's an awful thing, Trace, and I know it is, but instead of recommending that kid, I'd feel obliged to warn people against him—people who knew his father and would naturally want to step in and do something. I'd feel obliged to warn them. He's a thief . . ."

The moment this conversation was finished, Miss Rainey came in and stood by his desk. "I'm not going to be able to work for you any more, Mr. Weed," she said. "I can stay until the seventeenth if you need me, but I've been offered a whirlwind of a job, and I'd like to leave as soon as possible."

She went out, leaving him to face alone the wickedness of what he had done to the Thomas boy. His children in their photograph laughed and laughed, glazed with all the bright colors of summer, and he remembered that they had met a bagpiper on the beach that day and he had paid the piper a dollar to play them a battle song of the Black Watch. The girl would be at the house when he got home. He would spend another evening among his kind neighbors, picking and choosing dead-end streets, cart tracks, and the driveways of abandoned houses. There was nothing to mitigate his feeling—nothing that laughter or a game of softball with the children would change—and, thinking back over the plane crash, the Farquarsons' new maid, and Anne Murchison's difficulties with her drunken father, he wondered how he could have avoided arriving at just where he was. He was in trouble. He had been lost once in his life, coming back from a trout stream in the north woods, and he had now the same bleak realization that no amount of cheerfulness or hopefulness or valor or perseverance could help him find, in the gathering dark, the path that he'd lost. He smelled the forest. The feeling of bleakness was intolerable, and he saw clearly that he had reached the point where he would have to make a choice.

He could go to a psychiatrist, like Miss Rainey; he could go to church and confess his lusts; he could go to a Danish massage parlor in the West Seventies that had been recommended by a salesman; he could rape the girl or trust that he would somehow be prevented from doing this; or he could get drunk. It was his life, his boat, and, like every other man, he was made to be the father of thousands, and what harm could there be in a tryst that would make them both feel more kindly toward the world? This was the wrong train of thought, and he came back to the first, the psychiatrist. He had the telephone number of Miss Rainey's doctor, and he called and asked for an immediate appointment. He was insistent with the doctor's secretary—it was his manner in business—and when she said that the doctor's schedule was full for the next few weeks, Francis demanded an appointment that day and was told to come at five.

The psychiatrist's office was in a building that was used mostly by doctors and dentists, and the hallways were filled with the candy smell of mouthwash and memories of pain. Francis' character had been formed upon a series of private resolves—resolves about cleanliness, about going off the high diving board or repeating any other feat that challenged his courage, about punctuality, honesty, and virtue. To abdicate the perfect loneliness in which he had made his most vital decisions shattered his concept of character and left him now in a condition that felt like shock. He was stupefied. The scene for his *miserere mei Deus* was, like the waiting room of so many doctors' offices, a crude token gesture toward the sweets of domestic bliss: a place arranged with antiques, coffee tables, potted plants, and etchings of snow-covered bridges and geese in flight, although there were no children, no marriage bed, no stove, even, in this travesty of a house, where no one had ever spent the night and where the curtained windows looked straight onto a dark air shaft. Francis gave his name and address to a secretary and then saw, at the side of the room, a policeman moving toward him. "Hold it, hold it," the policeman said. "Don't move. Keep your hands where they are."

"I think it's all right, officer," the secretary began. "I think it will be—"

"Let's make sure," the policeman said, and he began to slap Francis' clothes, looking for what—pistols, knives, an icepick? Finding nothing, he went off, and the secretary began a nervous apology: "When you called on the telephone, Mr. Weed, you seemed very excited, and one of the doctor's patients has been threatening his life, and we have to be careful. If you want to go in now?" Francis pushed open a door connected to an electrical chime, and in the doctor's lair sat down heavily, blew his nose into a handkerchief, searched in his pockets for cigarettes, for matches, for something, and said hoarsely, with tears in his eyes, "I'm in love, Dr. Herzog."

It is a week or ten days later in Shady Hill. The seven-fourteen has come and gone, and here and there dinner is finished and the dishes are in the dish-washing machine. The village hangs, morally and economically, from a thread; but it hangs by its thread in the evening light. Donald Goslin has begun to worry the "Moonlight Sonata" again. *Marcato ma sempre pianissimo!* He seems to be wringing out a wet bath towel, but the housemaid does not heed him. She is writing a letter to Arthur Godfrey. In the cellar of his house, Francis Weed is building a coffee table. Dr. Herzog recommended woodwork as a therapy, and Francis finds some true consolation in the simple arithmetic involved and in the holy smell of new wood. Francis is happy. Upstairs, little Toby is crying, because he is tired. He puts off his cowboy hat, gloves, and fringed jacket, unbuckles the belt studded with gold and rubies, the silver bullets and holsters, slips off his suspenders, his checked shirt, and Levis, and sits on the edge of his bed to pull off his high boots. Leaving this equipment in a heap, he goes to the closet and takes his space suit off a nail. It is a struggle for him to get into the long tights, but he succeeds. He loops the magic cape over his shoulders and, climbing onto the footboard of his bed, he spreads his arms and flies the short distance to the floor, landing with a thump that is audible to everyone in the house but himself.

"Go home, Gertrude, go home," Mrs. Masterson says. "I told you to go home an hour ago, Gertrude. It's way past your suppertime, and your mother will be worried. Go home!" A door on the Babcocks' terrace flies open, and out comes Mrs. Babcock without any clothes on, pursued by her naked husband. (Their children are away at boarding school, and their terrace is screened by a hedge.) Over the terrace they go and in at the kitchen door, as passionate and handsome a nymph and satyr as you will find on any wall in Venice. Cutting the last of the roses in her garden, Julia hears old Mr. Nixon shouting at the squirrels in his bird-feeding station. "Rapscallions! Varmints! Avaunt and quit my sight!" A miserable cat wanders into the garden, sunk in spiritual and physical discomfort. Tied to its head is a small straw hat—a doll's hat—and it is securely buttoned into a doll's dress, from the skirts of which protrudes its long, hairy tail. As it walks, it shakes its feet, as if it had fallen into water.

"Here, pussy, pussy, pussy!" Julia calls.

"Here, pussy, here, poor pussy!" But the cat gives her a skeptical look and stumbles away in its skirts. The last to come is Jupiter. He prances through the tomato vines, holding in his generous mouth the remains of an evening slipper. Then it is dark; it is a night where kings in golden suits ride elephants over the mountains.

THE SORROWS OF GIN

✳ IT WAS a Sunday afternoon, and from her bedroom Amy could hear the Beardens coming in, followed a little while later by the Farquarsons and the Parminters. She went on reading *Black Beauty* until she felt in her bones that they might be eating something good. Then she closed her book and went down the stairs. The living-room door was shut, but through it she could hear the noise of loud talk and laughter. They must have been gossiping or worse, because they all stopped talking when she entered the room.

"Hi, Amy," Mr. Farquarson said.

"Mr. Farquarson spoke to you, Amy," her father said.

"Hello, Mr. Farquarson," she said. By standing outside the group for a minute, until they had resumed their conversation, and then by slipping past Mrs. Farquarson, she was able to swoop down on the nut dish and take a handful.

"Amy!" Mr. Lawton said.

"I'm sorry, Daddy," she said, retreating out of the circle, toward the piano.

"Put those nuts back," he said.

"I've handled them, Daddy," she said.

"Well, pass the nuts, dear," her mother said sweetly. "Perhaps someone else would like nuts."

Amy filled her mouth with the nuts she had taken, returned to the coffee table, and passed the nut dish.

"Thank you, Amy," they said, taking a peanut or two.

"How do you like your new school, Amy?" Mrs. Bearden asked.

"I like it," Amy said. "I like private schools better than public schools. It isn't so much like a factory."

"What grade are you in?" Mr. Bearden asked.

"Fourth," she said.

Her father took Mr. Parminter's glass and his own, and got up to go into the dining room and refill them. She fell into the chair he had left vacant.

"Don't sit in your father's chair, Amy," her mother said, not realizing that Amy's legs were worn out from riding a bicycle, while her father had done nothing but sit down all day.

As she walked toward the French doors, she heard her mother beginning to talk about the new cook. It was a good example of the interesting things they found to talk about.

"You'd better put your bicycle in the garage," her father said, returning with the fresh drinks. "It looks like rain."

Amy went out onto the terrace and looked at the sky, but it was not very cloudy, it wouldn't rain, and his advice, like all the advice he gave her, was superfluous. They were always at her. "Put your bicycle away." "Open the door for Grandmother, Amy." "Feed the cat." "Do your homework." "Pass the nuts." "Help Mrs. Bearden with her parcels." "Amy, please try and take more pains with your appearance."

They all stood, and her father came to the door and called her. "We're going over to the Parminters' for supper," he said. "Cook's here, so you won't be alone. Be sure and go to bed at eight like a good girl. And come and kiss me good night."

After their cars had driven off, Amy wandered through the kitchen to the cook's bedroom beyond it and knocked on the door. "Come in," a voice said, and when Amy entered, she found the cook, whose name was Rosemary, in her bathrobe, reading the Bible. Rosemary smiled at Amy. Her smile was sweet and her old eyes were blue. "Your parents have gone out again?" she asked. Amy said that they had, and the old woman invited her to sit down. "They do seem to enjoy themselves, don't they? During the four days I've been here, they've been out every night, or had people in." She put the Bible face down on her lap and smiled, but not at Amy. "Of course, the drinking that goes on here is all sociable, and what your parents do is none of my business, is it? I worry about drink more than most people, because of my poor sister. My poor sister drank too much. For ten years, I went to visit her on Sunday afternoons, and most of the time she was *non compos mentis*. Sometimes I'd find her huddled up on the floor with one or two sherry bottles empty beside her. Sometimes she'd seem sober enough to a stranger, but I could tell in a second by the way she spoke her words that she'd drunk enough not to be herself any more. Now my poor sister is gone, I don't have anyone to visit at all."

"What happened to your sister?" Amy asked.

"She was a lovely person, with a peaches-and-cream complexion and fair hair," Rosemary said. "Gin makes some

87

people gay—it makes them laugh and cry—but with my
sister it only made her sullen and withdrawn. When she was
drinking, she would retreat into herself. Drink made her
contrary. If I'd say the weather was fine, she'd tell me I was
wrong. If I'd say it was raining, she say it was clearing. She'd
correct me about everything I said, however small it was.
She died in Bellevue Hospital one summer when I was working in Maine. She was the only family I had."

The directness with which Rosemary spoke had the effect
on Amy of making her feel grown, and for once politeness
came to her easily. "You must miss your sister a great deal,"
she said.

"I was just sitting here now thinking about her. She was in
service, like me, and it's lonely work. You're always surrounded by a family, and yet you're never a part of it. Your
pride is often hurt. The Madams seem condescending and
inconsiderate. I'm not blaming the ladies I've worked for.
It's just in the nature of the relationship. They order chicken
salad, and you get up before dawn to get ahead of yourself,
and just as you've finished the chicken salad, they change
their minds and want crab-meat soup."

"My mother changes her mind all the time," Amy said.

"Sometimes you're in a country place with nobody else
in help. You're tired, but not too tired to feel lonely. You
go out onto the servants' porch when the pots and pans are
done, planning to enjoy God's creation, and although the
front of the house may have a fine view of the lake or the
mountains, the view from the back is never much. But there
is the sky and the trees and the stars and the birds singing and
the pleasure of resting your feet. But then you hear them in

the front of the house, laughing and talking with their guests and their sons and daughters. If you're new and they whisper, you can be sure they're talking about you. That takes all the pleasure out of the evening."

"Oh," Amy said.

"I've worked in all kinds of places—places where there were eight or nine in help and places where I was expected to burn the rubbish myself, on winter nights, and shovel the snow. In a house where there's a lot in help, there's usually some devil among them—some old butler or parlormaid— who tries to make your life miserable from the beginning. 'The Madam doesn't like it this way,' and 'The Madam doesn't like it that way,' and 'I've been with the Madam for twenty years,' they tell you. It takes a diplomat to get along. Then there is the rooms they give you, and every one of them I've ever seen is cheerless. If you have a bottle in your suitcase, it's a terrible temptation in the beginning not to take a drink to raise your spirits. But I have a strong character. It was different with my poor sister. She used to complain about nervousness, but, sitting here thinking about her to-night, I wonder if she suffered from nervousness at all. I wonder if she didn't make it all up. I wonder if she just wasn't meant to be in service. Toward the end, the only work she could get was out in the country, where nobody else would go, and she never lasted much more than a week or two. She'd take a little gin for her nervousness, then a little for her tiredness, and when she'd drunk her own bottle and everything she could steal, they'd hear about it in the front part of the house. There was usually a scene, and my poor sister always liked to have the last word. Oh, if I had had my

89

way, they'd be a law against it! It's not my business to advise you to take anything from your father, but I'd be proud of you if you'd empty his gin bottle into the sink now and then—the filthy stuff! But it's made me feel better to talk with you, sweetheart. It's made me not miss my poor sister so much. Now I'll read a little more in my Bible, and then I'll get you some supper."

The Lawtons had had a bad year with cooks—there had been five of them. The arrival of Rosemary had made Marcia Lawton think back to a vague theory of dispensations; she had suffered, and now she was being rewarded. Rosemary was clean, industrious, and cheerful, and her table—as the Lawtons said—was just like the Chambord. On Wednesday night after dinner, she took the train to New York, promising to return on the evening train Thursday. Thursday morning, Marcia went into the cook's room. It was a distasteful but a habitual precaution. The absence of anything personal in the room—a package of cigarettes, a fountain pen, an alarm clock, a radio, or anything else that could tie the old woman to the place—gave her the uneasy feeling that she was being deceived, as she had so often been deceived by cooks in the past. She opened the closet door and saw a single uniform hanging there and, on the closet floor, Rosemary's old suitcase and the white shoes she wore in the kitchen. The suitcase was locked, but when Marcia lifted it, it seemed to be nearly empty.

Mr. Lawton and Amy drove to the station after dinner on Thursday to meet the eight-sixteen train. The top of the car was down, and the brisk air, the starlight, and the company of her father made the little girl feel kindly toward the world. The railroad station in Shady Hill resembled the railroad stations in old movies she had seen on television, where detectives and spies, bluebeards and their trusting victims, were met to be driven off to remote country estates. Amy liked the station, particularly toward dark. She imagined that the people who traveled on the locals were engaged on errands that were more urgent and sinister than commuting. Except when there was a heavy fog or a snowstorm, the club car that her father traveled on seemed to have the gloss and the monotony of the rest of his life. The locals that ran at odd hours belonged to a world of deeper contrasts, where she would like to live.

They were a few minutes early, and Amy got out of the car and stood on the platform. She wondered what the fringe of string that hung above the tracks at either end of the station was for, but she knew enough not to ask her father, because he wouldn't be able to tell her. She could hear the train before it came into view, and the noise excited her and made her happy. When the train drew in to the station and stopped, she looked in the lighted windows for Rosemary and didn't see her. Mr. Lawton got out of the car and joined Amy on the platform. They could see the conductor bending over someone in a seat, and finally the cook rose. She clung to the conductor as he led her out to the platform of the car, and she was crying. "Like peaches and cream," Amy heard her sob. "A lovely, lovely person." The conductor spoke to her kindly, put his arm around her shoulders, and eased her down the steps. Then the train pulled out, and she stood there drying her tears. "Don't say a word, Mr. Lawton," she said, "and I won't say anything." She held out a small paper bag. "Here's a present for you, little girl."

"Thank you, Rosemary," Amy said. She looked into the paper bag and saw that it contained several packets of Japanese water flowers.

Rosemary walked toward the car with the caution of someone who can hardly find the way in the dim light. A sour smell came from her. Her best coat was spotted with mud and ripped in the back. Mr. Lawton told Amy to get in the back seat of the car, and made the cook sit in front, beside him. He slammed the car door shut after her angrily, and then went around to the driver's seat and drove home. Rosemary reached into her handbag and took out a Coca-Cola bottle with a cork stopper and took a drink. Amy could tell by the smell that the Coca-Cola bottle was filled with gin.

"Rosemary!" Mr. Lawton said.

"I'm lonely," the cook said. "I'm lonely, and I'm afraid, and it's all I've got."

He said nothing more until he had turned in to their drive and brought the car around to the back door. "Go and get your suitcase, Rosemary," he said. "I'll wait here in the car."

As soon as the cook had staggered into the house, he told Amy to go in by the front door. "Go upstairs to your room and get ready for bed."

Her mother called down the stairs when Amy came in, to ask if Rosemary had returned. Amy didn't answer. She went to the bar, took an open gin bottle, and emptied it into the pantry sink. She was nearly crying when she encountered her mother in the living room, and told her that her father was taking the cook back to the station.

When Amy came home from school the next day, she found a heavy, black-haired woman cleaning the living room. The car Mr. Lawton usually drove to the station was at the garage for a checkup, and Amy drove to the station with her mother to meet him. As he came across the station platform, she could tell, by the lack of color in his face, that he had had a hard day. He kissed her mother, touched Amy on the head, and got behind the wheel.

"You know," her mother said, "there's something terribly wrong with the guest-room shower."

"Damn it, Marcia," he said, "I wish you wouldn't always greet me with bad news!"

His grating voice oppressed Amy, and she began to fiddle with the button that raised and lowered the window.

"Stop that, Amy!" he said.

"Oh, well, the shower isn't important," her mother said. She laughed weakly.

"When I got back from San Francisco last week," he said, "you couldn't wait to tell me that we need a new oil burner."

"Well, I've got a part-time cook. That's good news."

"Is she a lush?" her father asked.

"Don't be disagreeable, dear. She'll get us some dinner and wash the dishes and take the bus home. We're going to the Farquarsons'."

"I'm really too tired to go anywhere," he said.

"Who's going to take care of me?" Amy asked.

"You always have a good time at the Farquarsons'," her mother said.

"Well, let's leave early," he said.

"Who's going to take care of me?" Amy asked.

"Mrs. Henlein," her mother said.

When they got home, Amy went over to the piano.

Her father washed his hands in the bathroom off the hall and then went to the bar. He came into the living room holding the empty gin bottle. "What's her name?" he asked.

"Ruby," her mother said.

"She's exceptional. She's drunk a quart of gin on her first day."

"Oh dear!" her mother said. "Well, let's not make any trouble now."

"Everybody is drinking my liquor," her father shouted, "and I am God-damned sick and tired of it!"

"There's plenty of gin in the closet," her mother said. "Open another bottle."

"We paid that gardener three dollars an hour and all he did was sneak in here and drink up my Scotch. The sitter we had before we got Mrs. Henlein used to water my bourbon, and I don't have to remind you about Rosemary. The cook before Rosemary not only drank everything in my liquor cabinet but she drank all the rum, kirsch, sherry, and wine that we had in the kitchen for cooking. Then, there's that Polish woman we had last summer. Even that old laundress. *And* the painters. I think they must put some kind of a mark on my door. I think the agency must have checked me off as an easy touch."

"Well, let's get through dinner, and then you can speak to her."

"The hell with that!" he said. "I'm not going to encourage people to rob me. *Ruby!*" He shouted her name several times, but she didn't answer. Then she appeared in the dining-room doorway, wearing her hat and coat.

"I'm sick," she said. Amy could see that she was frightened.

"I should think you would be," her father said.

"I'm sick," the cook mumbled, "and I can't find anything around here, and I'm going home."

"Good," he said. "Good! I'm through with paying people to come in here and drink my liquor."

The cook started out the front way, and Marcia Lawton followed her into the front hall to pay her something. Amy had watched this scene from the piano bench, a position that was withdrawn but that still gave her a good view. She saw her father get a fresh bottle of gin and make a shaker of Martinis. He looked very unhappy.

"Well," her mother said when she came back into the room. "You know, she didn't look drunk."

"Please don't argue with me, Marcia," her father said. He poured two cocktails, said, "Cheers," and drank a little. "We can get some dinner at Orfeo's," he said.

"I suppose so," her mother said. "I'll rustle up something for Amy." She went into the kitchen, and Amy opened her music to "Reflets d'Automne." "COUNT," her music teacher had written. "COUNT and lightly, lightly . . ." Amy began to play. Whenever she made a mistake, she said "Darn it!" and started at the beginning again. In the middle of "Reflets d'Automne" it struck her that *she* was the one who had emptied the gin bottle. Her perplexity was so intense that she stopped playing, but her feelings did not go beyond perplexity, although she did not have the strength to continue playing the piano. Her mother relieved her. "Your supper's in the kitchen, dear," she said. "And you can take a popsicle out of the deep freeze for dessert. Just one."

Marcia Lawton held her empty glass toward her husband, who filled it from the shaker. Then she went upstairs. Mr. Lawton remained in the room, and, studying her father closely, Amy saw that his tense look had begun to soften. He did not seem so unhappy any more, and as she passed him on her way to the kitchen, he smiled at her tenderly and patted her on the top of the head.

When Amy had finished her supper, eaten her popsicle, and exploded the bag it came in, she returned to the piano and played "Chopsticks" for a while. Her father came downstairs in his evening clothes, put his drink on the mantelpiece, and went to the French doors to look at his terrace and his garden. Amy noticed that the transformation that had begun with a softening of his features was even more advanced. At last, he seemed happy. Amy wondered if he was drunk, although his walk was not unsteady. If anything, it was more steady.

Her parents never achieved the kind of rolling, swinging gait that she saw impersonated by a tightrope walker in the circus each year while the band struck up "Show Me the Way to Go Home" and that she liked to imitate herself sometimes. She liked to turn round and round and round on the lawn, until, staggering and a little sick, she would whoop, "I'm drunk! I'm a drunken man!" and reel over the grass, righting herself as she was about to fall and finding herself not unhappy at having lost for a second her ability to see the world. But she had never seen her parents like that. She had never seen them hanging on to a lamppost and singing and reeling, but she had seen them fall down. They were never indecorous

—they seemed to get more decorous and formal the more they drank—but sometimes her father would get up to fill everybody's glass and he would walk straight enough but his shoes would seem to stick to the carpet. And sometimes, when he got to the dining-room door, he would miss it by a foot or more. Once, she had seen him walk into the wall with such force that he collapsed onto the floor and broke most of the glasses he was carrying. One or two people laughed, but the laughter was not general or hearty, and most of them pretended that he had not fallen down at all. When her father got to his feet, he went right on to the bar as if nothing had happened. Amy had once seen Mrs. Farquarson miss the chair she was about to sit in, by a foot, and thump down onto the floor, but nobody laughed then, and they pretended that Mrs. Farquarson hadn't fallen down at all. They seemed like actors in a play. In the school play, when you knocked over a paper tree you were supposed to pick it up without showing what you were doing, so that you would not spoil the illusion of being in a deep forest, and that was the way *they* were when somebody fell down.

Now her father had that stiff, funny walk that was so different from the way he tramped up and down the station platform in the morning, and she could see that he was looking for something. He was looking for his drink. It was right on the mantelpiece, but he didn't look there. He looked on all the tables in the living room. Then he went out onto the terrace and looked there, and then he came back into the living room and looked on all the tables again. Then he went back onto the terrace, and then back over the living-room tables, looking three times in the same place, although he

97

was always telling her to look intelligently when she lost her sneakers or her raincoat. "Look for it, Amy," he was always saying. "Try and remember where you left it. I can't buy you a new raincoat every time it rains." Finally he gave up and poured himself a cocktail in another glass. "I'm going to get Mrs. Henlein," he told Amy, as if this were an important piece of information.

Amy's only feeling for Mrs. Henlein was indifference, and when her father returned with the sitter, Amy thought of the nights, stretching into weeks—the years, almost—when she had been cooped up with Mrs. Henlein. Mrs. Henlein was very polite and was always telling Amy what was ladylike and what was not. Mrs. Henlein also always wanted to know where Amy's parents were going and what kind of a party it was, although it was none of her business. She always sat down on the sofa as if she owned the place, and talked about people she had never even been introduced to, and asked Amy to bring her the newspaper, although she had no authority at all.

When Marcia Lawton came down, Mrs. Henlein wished her good evening. "Have a lovely party," she called after the Lawtons as they went out the door. Then she turned to Amy. "Where are your parents going, sweetheart?"

"I don't know," Amy said.

"But you must know, sweetheart. Put on your thinking cap and try and remember. Are they going to the club?"

"No," Amy said.

"I wonder if they could be going to the Trenchers'," Mrs. Henlein said. "The Trenchers' house was lighted up when we came by."

"They're not going to the Trenchers'," Amy said. "They hate the Trenchers."

"Well, where are they going, sweetheart?" Mrs. Henlein asked.

"They're going to the Farquarsons'," Amy said.

"Well, that's all I wanted to know, sweetheart," Mrs. Henlein said. "Now get me the newspaper and hand it to me politely. *Politely,*" she said, as Amy approached her with the paper. "It don't mean anything when you do things for your elders unless you do them politely." She put on her glasses and began to read the paper.

Amy went upstairs to her room. In a glass on her table were the Japanese flowers that Rosemary had brought her, blooming stalely in water that was colored pink from the dyes. Amy went down the back stairs and through the kitchen into the dining room. Her father's cocktail things were spread over the bar. She emptied the gin bottle into the pantry sink and then put it back where she had found it. It was too late to ride her bicycle and too early to go to bed, and she knew that if she got anything interesting on the television, like a murder, Mrs. Henlein would make her turn it off. Then she remembered that her father had brought her home from his trip West a book about horses, and she ran cheerfully up the back stairs to read her new book.

It was after two when the Lawtons returned. Mrs. Henlein, asleep on the living-room sofa dreaming about a dusty attic, was awakened by their voices in the hall. Marcia Lawton paid her, and thanked her, and asked if anyone had called, and then went upstairs. Mr. Lawton was in the dining room, rattling the bottles around. Mrs. Henlein, anxious to get into her own bed and back to sleep, prayed that he wasn't going to pour himself another drink, as they so often did. She was driven home night after night by drunken gentlemen. He stood in the door of the dining room, holding an empty bottle in his hand. "You must be stinking, Mrs. Henlein," he said.

"Hmm," she said. She didn't understand.

"You drank a full quart of gin," he said.

The lackluster old woman—half between wakefulness and sleep—gathered together her bones and groped for her gray hair. It was in her nature to collect stray cats, pile the bathroom up to the ceiling with interesting and valuable newspapers, rouge, talk to herself, sleep in her underwear in case of fire, quarrel over the price of soup bones, and have it circulated around the neighborhood that when she finally died in her dusty junk heap, the mattress would be full of bankbooks and the pillow stuffed with hundred-dollar bills. She had resisted all these rich temptations in order to appear a lady, and she was repaid by being called a common thief. She began to scream at him.

"You take that back, Mr. Lawton! You take back every one of those words you just said! I never stole anything in my whole life, and nobody in my family ever stole anything, and I don't have to stand here and be insulted by a drunk man. Why, as for drinking, I haven't drunk enough to fill an eyeglass for twenty-five years. Mr. Henlein took me to a place of refreshment twenty-five years ago, and I drank two Manhattan cocktails that made me so sick and dizzy that I've never liked the stuff ever since. How dare you speak to me like this! Calling me a thief and a drunken woman! Oh, you disgust me—you disgust me in your ignorance of all the trouble I've had. Do you know what I had for Christmas dinner last year? I had a bacon sandwich. Son of a bitch!" She began to weep. "I'm glad I said it!" she screamed. "It's the first time I've used a dirty word in my whole life and I'm glad I said it. Son of a bitch!" A sense of liberation, as if she stood at the bow of a great ship, came over her. "I lived in this neighborhood my whole life. I can remember when it was full of good farming people and there was fish in the rivers. My father had four acres of sweet meadowland and a name that was known far and wide, and on my mother's side I'm descended from patroons, Dutch nobility. My mother was the spit and image of Queen Wilhelmina. You think you can get away with insulting me, but you're very, very, very much mistaken." She went to the telephone and, picking up the receiver, screamed, "Police! Police! Police! This is Mrs. Henlein, and I'm over at the Lawtons'. He's drunk, and he's calling me insulting names, and I want you to come over here and arrest him!"

The voices woke Amy, and, lying in her bed, she perceived vaguely the pitiful corruption of the adult world; how crude and frail it was, like a piece of worn burlap, patched with stupidities and mistakes, useless and ugly, and yet they never saw its worthlessness, and when you pointed it out to them, they were indignant. But as the voices went on and she heard the cry "Police! Police!" she was frightened. She did not see how they could arrest her, although they could find her fingerprints on the empty bottle, but it was not her own danger that frightened her but the collapse, in the middle of the night, of her father's house. It was all her fault, and when she heard her father speaking into the extension telephone in the library, she felt sunk in guilt. Her father tried to be good and kind—oh, she knew he never meant to be anything else—and, remembering the expensive illustrated book about horses that he had brought her from the West, she had to set her teeth to keep from crying. She covered her head with a pillow and realized miserably that she would have to go away. She had plenty of friends from the time when they used to live in New York, or she could spend the night in the Park or hide in a museum. She would have to go away.

"Good morning," her father said at breakfast. "Ready for a good day!" Cheered by the swelling light in the sky, by the recollection of the manner in which he had handled Mrs. Henlein and kept the police from coming, refreshed by his sleep, and pleased at the thought of playing golf, Mr. Lawton spoke with feeling, but the words seemed to Amy offensive and fatuous; they took away her appetite, and she slumped over her cereal bowl, stirring it with a spoon. "Don't slump, Amy," he said. Then she remembered the night, the screaming, the resolve to go. His cheerfulness refreshed her memory. Her decision was settled. She had a ballet lesson at ten, and she was going to have lunch with Lillian Towele. Then she would leave.

Children prepare for a sea voyage with a toothbrush and a Teddy bear; they equip themselves for a trip around the world with a pair of odd socks, a conch shell, and a thermometer; books and stones and peacock feathers, candy bars, tennis balls, soiled handkerchiefs, and skeins of old string appear to them to be the necessities of travel, and Amy packed, that afternoon, with the impulsiveness of her kind. She was late coming home from lunch, and her getaway was delayed, but she didn't mind. She could catch one of the late-afternoon locals; one of the cooks' trains. Her father was playing golf and her mother was off somewhere. A part-time worker was cleaning the living room. When Amy had finished packing, she went into her parents' bathroom and flushed the toilet. While the water murmured, she took a twenty-dollar bill from her mother's desk. Then she went downstairs and left the house and walked around Blenhollow Circle and down Alewives Lane to the station. No regrets or good-bys formed in her mind. She went over the names of the friends she had in the city, in case she decided not to spend the night in a museum. When she opened the door of the waiting room, Mr. Flanagan, the stationmaster, was poking his coal fire.

"I want to buy a ticket to New York," Amy said.

"One-way or round-trip?"

"One-way, please."

Mr. Flanagan went through the door into the ticket office and raised the glass window. "I'm afraid I haven't got a half-fare ticket for you, Amy," he said. "I'll have to write one."

"That's all right," she said. She put the twenty-dollar bill on the counter.

"And in order to change that," he said, "I'll have to go over to the other side. Here's the four-thirty-two coming in now, but you'll be able to get the five-ten." She didn't protest, and went and sat beside her cardboard suitcase, which was printed with European hotel and place names. When the local had come and gone, Mr. Flanagan shut his glass window and walked over the footbridge to the northbound platform and called the Lawtons'. Mr. Lawton had just come in from his game and was mixing himself a cocktail. "I think your daughter's planning to take some kind of a trip," Mr. Flanagan said.

It was dark by the time Mr. Lawton got down to the station. He saw his daughter through the station window. The girl sitting on the bench, the rich names on her paper suitcase, touched him as it was in her power to touch him only when she seemed helpless or when she was very sick. Someone had walked over his grave! He shivered with longing, he felt his skin coarsen as when, driving home late and alone, a shower of leaves on the wind crossed the beam of his headlights, liberating him for a second at the most from the literal symbols of his life—the buttonless shirts, the vouchers and bank statements, the order blanks, and the empty glasses. He seemed to listen—God knows for what. Commands, drums, the crackle of signal fires, the music of the glockenspiel—how sweet it sounds on the Alpine air— singing from a tavern in the pass, the honking of wild swans; he seemed to smell the salt air in the churches of Venice. Then, as it was with the leaves, the power of her figure to trouble him was ended; his gooseflesh vanished. He was himself. Oh, why should she want to run away? Travel—and who knew better than a man who spent three days of every fortnight on the road—was a world of overheated plane cabins and repetitious magazines, where even the coffee, even the champagne, tasted of plastics. How could he teach her that home sweet home was the best place of all?

THE WORM IN THE APPLE

✳ **THE CRUTCHMANS** were so very, very happy and so temperate in all their habits and so pleased with everything that came their way that one was bound to suspect a worm in their rosy apple and that the extraordinary rosiness of the fruit was only meant to conceal the gravity and the depth of the infection. Their house, for instance, on Hill Street with all those big glass windows. Who but someone suffering from a guilt complex would want so much light to pour into their rooms? And all the wall-to-wall carpeting as if an inch of bare floor (there was none) would touch on some deep memory of unrequition and loneliness. And there was a certain necrophilic ardor to their gardening. Why be so intense about digging holes and planting seeds and watching them come up? Why this morbid concern with the earth? She was a pretty woman with that striking pallor you so often find in nymphomaniacs. Larry was a big man who used to garden without a shirt, which may have shown a tendency to infantile exhibitionism.

They moved happily out to Shady Hill after the war. Larry had served in the Navy. They had two happy children:

Rachel and Tom. But there were already some clouds on their horizon. Larry's ship had been sunk in the war and he had spent four days on a raft in the Mediterranean and surely this experience would make him skeptical about the comforts and songbirds of Shady Hill and leave him with some racking nightmares. But what was perhaps more serious was the fact that Helen was rich. She was the only daughter of old Charlie Simpson—one of the last of the industrial buccaneers—who had left her with a larger income than Larry would ever take away from his job at Melcher & Thaw. The dangers in this situation are well-known. Since Larry did not have to make a living—since he lacked any incentive—he might take it easy, spend too much time on the golf links and always have a glass in his hand. Helen would confuse financial with emotional independence and damage the delicate balances within their marriage. But Larry seemed to have no nightmares and Helen spread her income among the charities and lived a comfortable but a modest life. Larry went to his job each morning with such enthusiasm that you might think he was trying to escape from something. His participation in the life of the community was so vigorous that he must have been left with almost no time for self-examination. He was everywhere: he was at the communion rail, the fifty-yard line, he played the oboe with the Chamber Music Club, drove the fire truck, served on the school board and rode the 8:03 into New York every morning. What was the sorrow that drove him?

He may have wanted a larger family. Why did they only have two children? Why not three or four? Was there perhaps some breakdown in their relationship after the birth of Tom? Rachel, the oldest, was terribly fat when she was a girl and quite aggressive in a mercenary way. Every spring she would drag an old dressing table out of the garage and set it up on the sidewalk with a sign saying: FReSH LEMonADE. 15¢. Tom had pneumonia when he was six and nearly died but he recovered and there were no visible complications. The children may have felt rebellious about the conformity of their parents for they were exacting conformists. Two cars? Yes. Did they go to church? Every single Sunday they got to their knees and prayed with ardor. Clothing? They couldn't have been more punctilious in their observance of the sumptuary laws. Book clubs, local art and music lovers associations, athletics and cards—they were up to their necks in everything. But if the children were rebellious they concealed their rebellion and seemed happily to love their parents and happily to be loved in return, but perhaps there was in this love the ruefulness of some deep disappointment. Perhaps he was impotent. Perhaps she was frigid—but hardly, with that pallor. Everyone in the community with wandering hands had given them both a try but they had all been put off. What was the source of this constancy? Were they frightened? Were they prudish? Were they monogamous? What was at the bottom of this appearance of happiness?

As their children grew one might look to them for the worm in the apple. They would be rich, they would inherit Helen's fortune and we might see here, moving over them, the shadow that so often falls upon children who can count on a lifetime of financial security. And anyhow Helen loved her son much too much. She bought him everything he wanted. Driving him to dancing school in his first blue serge suit she was so entranced by the manly figure he cut as he climbed the stairs that she drove the car straight into an

109

elm tree. Such an infatuation was bound to lead to trouble. And if she favored her son she was bound to discriminate against her daughter. Listen to her. "Rachel's feet," she says, "are immense, simply immense. I can never get shoes for her." Now perhaps we see the worm. Like most beautiful women she is jealous; she is jealous of her own daughter! She cannot brook competition. She will dress the girl in hideous clothing, have her hair curled in some unbecoming way and keep talking about the size of her feet until the poor girl will refuse to go to the dances or if she is forced to go she will sulk in the ladies' room, staring at her monstrous feet. She will become so wretched and so lonely that in order to express herself she will fall in love with an unstable poet and fly with him to Rome, where they will live out a miserable and a boozy exile. But when the girl enters the room she is pretty and prettily dressed and she smiles at her mother with perfect love. Her feet are quite large, to be sure, but so is her front. Perhaps we should look to the son to find our trouble.

And there is trouble. He fails his junior year in high school and has to repeat and as a result of having to repeat he feels alienated from the members of his class and is put, by chance, at a desk next to Carrie Witchell, who is the most conspicuous dish in Shady Hill. Everyone knows about the Witchells and their pretty, high-spirited daughter. They drink too much and live in one of those frame houses in Maple Dell. The girl is really beautiful and everyone knows how her shrewd old parents are planning to climb out of Maple Dell on the strength of her white, white skin. What a perfect situation! They will know about Helen's wealth. In the darkness of their bedroom they will calculate the settlement they can demand and in the malodorous kitchen where they take all their meals they will tell their pretty daughter to let the boy go as far as he wants. But Tom fell out of love with Carrie as swiftly as he fell into it and after that he fell in love with Karen Strawbridge and Susie Morris and Anna Macken and you might think that he was unstable, but in his second year in college he announced his engagement to Elizabeth Trustman and they were married after his graduation and since he then had to serve his time in the army she followed him to his post in Germany, where they studied and learned the language and befriended the people and were a credit to their country.

Rachel's way was not so easy. When she lost her fat she became very pretty and quite fast. She smoked and drank and probably fornicated and the abyss that opens up before a pretty and an intemperate young woman is unfathomable. What, but chance, was there to keep her from ending up as a hostess in a Times Square dance hall? And what would her poor father think, seeing the face of his daughter, her breasts lightly covered with gauze, gazing mutely at him on a rainy morning from one of those show cases? What she did was to fall in love with the son of the Farquarsons' German gardener. He had come with his family to the United States on the Displaced Persons quota after the war. His name was Eric Reiner and to be fair about it he was an exceptional young man who looked on the United States as a truly New World. The Crutchmans must have been sad about Rachel's choice—not to say heartbroken—but they concealed their feelings. The Reiners did not. This hard-working German couple thought the marriage hopeless and improper. At one point the father beat his son over the head with a stick of firewood. But the young couple continued to see each other and presently they eloped. They had to. Rachel was three months pregnant. Eric was then a freshman at Tufts, where he had a scholarship. Helen's money came in handy here and she was able to rent an apartment in Boston for the young couple and pay their expenses. That their first grandchild was premature did not seem to bother the Crutchmans. When Eric graduated from college he got a fellowship at M.I.T. and took his Ph.D. in physics and was taken on as an associate in the department. He could have gone into industry at a higher salary but he liked to teach and Rachel was happy in Cambridge, where they remained.

With their own dear children gone away the Crutchmans might be expected to suffer the celebrated spiritual destitution of their age and their kind—the worm in the apple would at last be laid bare—although watching this charming couple as they entertained their friends or read the books they enjoyed one might wonder if the worm was not in the eye of the observer who, through timidity or moral cowardice, could not embrace the broad range of their natural enthusiasms and would not grant that, while Larry played neither Bach nor football very well, his pleasure in both was genuine. You might at least expect to see in them the usual destructiveness of time, but either through luck or as a result of their temperate and healthy lives they had lost neither their teeth nor their hair. The touchstone of their euphoria remained potent, and while Larry gave up the fire truck he could still be seen at the communion rail, the fifty-yard line, the 8:03 and the Chamber Music Club, and through the prudence and shrewdness of Helen's broker they got richer and richer and richer and lived happily, happily, happily, happily.

THE FIVE-FORTY-EIGHT

✻ **WHEN BLAKE** stepped out of the elevator, he saw her. A few people, mostly men waiting for girls, stood in the lobby watching the elevator doors. She was among them. As he saw her, her face took on a look of such loathing and purpose that he realized she had been waiting for him. He did not approach her. She had no legitimate business with him. They had nothing to say. He turned and walked toward the glass doors at the end of the lobby, feeling that faint guilt and bewilderment we experience when we by-pass some old friend or classmate who seems threadbare, or sick, or miserable in some other way. It was five-eighteen by the clock in the Western Union office. He could catch the express. As he waited his turn at the revolving doors, he saw that it was still raining. It had been raining all day, and he noticed now how much louder the rain made the noises of the street. Outside, he started walking briskly east toward Madison Avenue. Traffic was tied up, and horns were blowing urgently on a crosstown street in the distance. The sidewalk was crowded. He wondered what she had hoped to gain by a glimpse of him coming out of the office building at the end of the day. Then

115

he wondered if she was following him.

Walking in the city, we seldom turn and look back. The habit restrained Blake. He listened for a minute—foolishly—as he walked, as if he could distinguish her footsteps from the worlds of sound in the city at the end of a rainy day. Then he noticed, ahead of him on the other side of the street, a break in the wall of buildings. Something had been torn down; something was being put up, but the steel structure had only just risen above the sidewalk fence and daylight poured through the gap. Blake stopped opposite here and looked into a store window. It was a decorator's or an auctioneer's. The window was arranged like a room in which people live and entertain their friends. There were cups on the coffee table, magazines to read, and flowers in the vases, but the flowers were dead and the cups were empty and the guests had not come. In the plate glass, Blake saw a clear reflection of himself and the crowds that were passing, like shadows, at his back. Then he saw her image—so close to him that it shocked him. She was standing only a foot or two behind him. He could have turned then and asked her what she wanted, but instead of recognizing her, he shied away abruptly from the reflection of her contorted face and went along the street. She might be meaning to do him harm—she might be meaning to kill him.

The suddenness with which he moved when he saw the reflection of her face tipped the water out of his hatbrim in such a way that some of it ran down his neck. It felt unpleasantly like the sweat of fear. Then the cold water falling into his face and onto his bare hands, the rancid smell of the wet gutters and pavings, the knowledge that his feet

were beginning to get wet and that he might catch cold—
all the common discomforts of walking in the rain—seemed
to heighten the menace of his pursuer and to give him a
morbid consciousness of his own physicalness and of the
ease with which he could be hurt. He could see ahead of him
the corner of Madison Avenue, where the lights were
brighter. He felt that if he could get to Madison Avenue he
would be all right. At the corner, there was a bakery shop
with two entrances, and he went in by the door on the crosstown street, bought a coffee ring, like any other commuter,
and went out the Madison Avenue door. As he started down
Madison Avenue, he saw her waiting for him by a hut where
newspapers were sold.

She was not clever. She would be easy to shake. He could
get into a taxi by one door and leave by the other. He could
speak to a policeman. He could run—although he was afraid
that if he did run, it might precipitate the violence he now
felt sure she had planned. He was approaching a part of the
city that he knew well and where the maze of street-level
and underground passages, elevator banks, and crowded
lobbies made it easy for a man to lose a pursuer. The thought
of this, and a whiff of sugary warmth from the coffee ring,
cheered him. It was absurd to imagine being harmed on a
crowded street. She was foolish, misled, lonely perhaps—
that was all it could amount to. He was an insignificant man,
and there was no point in anyone's following him from his
office to the station. He knew no secrets of any consequence.
The reports in his brief case had no bearing on war, peace,
the dope traffic, the hydrogen bomb, or any of the other inter-
national skulduggeries that he associated with pursuers, men

117

in trench coats, and wet sidewalks. Then he saw ahead of him the door of a men's bar. Oh, it was so simple!

He ordered a Gibson and shouldered his way in between two other men at the bar, so that if she should be watching from the window she would lose sight of him. The place was crowded with commuters putting down a drink before the ride home. They had brought in on their clothes—on their shoes and umbrellas—the rancid smell of the wet dusk outside, but Blake began to relax as soon as he tasted his Gibson and looked around at the common, mostly not-young faces that surrounded him and that were worried, if they were worried at all, about tax rates and who would be put in charge of merchandising. He tried to remember her name—Miss Dent, Miss Bent, Miss Lent—and he was surprised to find that he could not remember it, although he was proud of the retentiveness and reach of his memory and it had only been six months ago.

Personnel had sent her up one afternoon—he was looking for a secretary. He saw a dark woman—in her twenties, perhaps—who was slender and shy. Her dress was simple, her figure was not much, one of her stockings was crooked, but her voice was soft and he had been willing to try her out. After she had been working for him a few days, she told him that she had been in the hospital for eight months and that it had been hard after this for her to find work, and she wanted to thank him for giving her a chance. Her hair was dark, her eyes were dark; she left with him a pleasant impression of darkness. As he got to know her better, he felt that she was oversensitive and, as a consequence, lonely. Once, when she was speaking to him of what she imagined

118

his life to be—full of friendships, money, and a large and loving family—he had thought he recognized a peculiar feeling of deprivation. She seemed to imagine the lives of the rest of the world to be more brilliant than they were. Once, she had put a rose on his desk, and he had dropped it into the wastebasket. "I don't like roses," he told her.

She had been competent, punctual, and a good typist, and he had found only one thing in her that he could object to—her handwriting. He could not associate the crudeness of her handwriting with her appearance. He would have expected her to write a rounded backhand, and in her writing there were intermittent traces of this, mixed with clumsy printing. Her writing gave him the feeling that she had been the victim of some inner—some emotional—conflict that had in its violence broken the continuity of the lines she was able to make on paper. When she had been working for him three weeks—no longer—they stayed late one night and he offered, after work, to buy her a drink. "If you really want a drink," she said, "I have some whiskey at my place."

She lived in a room that seemed to him like a closet. There were suit boxes and hatboxes piled in a corner, and although the room seemed hardly big enough to hold the bed, the dresser, and the chair he sat in, there was an upright piano against one wall, with a book of Beethoven sonatas on the rack. She gave him a drink and said that she was going to put on something more comfortable. He urged her to; that was, after all, what he had come for. If he had had any qualms, they would have been practical. Her diffidence, the feeling of deprivation in her point of view, promised to protect him from any consequences. Most of the many women

119

he had known had been picked for their lack of self-esteem.

When he put on his clothes again, an hour or so later, she was weeping. He felt too contented and warm and sleepy to worry much about her tears. As he was dressing, he noticed on the dresser a note she had written to a cleaning woman. The only light came from the bathroom—the door was ajar—and in this half light the hideously scrawled letters again seemed entirely wrong for her, and as if they must be the handwriting of some other and very gross woman. The next day, he did what he felt was the only sensible thing. When she was out for lunch, he called personnel and asked them to fire her. Then he took the afternoon off. A few days later, she came to the office, asking to see him. He told the switchboard girl not to let her in. He had not seen her again until this evening.

Blake drank a second Gibson and saw by the clock that he had missed the express. He would get the local—the five-forty-eight. When he left the bar the sky was still light; it was still raining. He looked carefully up and down the street and saw that the poor woman had gone. Once or twice, he looked over his shoulder, walking to the station, but he seemed to be safe. He was still not quite himself, he realized, because he had left his coffee ring at the bar, and he was not a man who forgot things. This lapse of memory pained him.

He bought a paper. The local was only half full when he boarded it, and he got a seat on the river side and took off his raincoat. He was a slender man with brown hair—undistinguished in every way, unless you could have divined in his pallor or his gray eyes his unpleasant tastes. He dressed —like the rest of us—as if he admitted the existence of sump-

tuary laws. His raincoat was the pale buff color of a mush-
room. His hat was dark brown; so was his suit. Except for
the few bright threads in his necktie, there was a scrupulous
lack of color in his clothing that seemed protective.

He looked around the car for neighbors. Mrs. Compton
was several seats in front of him, to the right. She smiled, but
her smile was fleeting. It died swiftly and horribly. Mr.
Watkins was directly in front of Blake. Mr. Watkins needed
a haircut, and he had broken the sumptuary laws; he was
wearing a corduroy jacket. He and Blake had quarreled, so
they did not speak.

The swift death of Mrs. Compton's smile did not affect
Blake at all. The Comptons lived in the house next to the
Blakes, and Mrs. Compton had never understood the im-
portance of minding her own business. Louise Blake took her
troubles to Mrs. Compton, Blake knew, and instead of discouraging her crying jags, Mrs. Compton had come to
imagine herself a sort of confessor and had developed a lively
curiosity about the Blakes' intimate affairs. She had probably
been given an account of their most recent quarrel. Blake
had come home one night, overworked and tired, and had
found that Louise had done nothing about getting supper.
He had gone into the kitchen, followed by Louise, and he had
pointed out to her that the date was the fifth. He had drawn
a circle around the date on the kitchen calendar. "One week
is the twelfth," he had said. "Two weeks will be the nineteenth." He drew a circle around the nineteenth. "I'm not
going to speak to you for two weeks," he had said. "That
will be the nineteenth." She had wept, she had protested, but
it had been eight or ten years since she had been able to

121

touch him with her entreaties. Louise had got old. Now the lines in her face were ineradicable, and when she clapped her glasses onto her nose to read the evening paper she looked to him like an unpleasant stranger. The physical charms that had been her only attraction were gone. It had been nine years since Blake had built a bookshelf in the doorway that connected their rooms and had fitted into the bookshelf wooden doors that could be locked, since he did not want the children to see his books. But their prolonged estrangement didn't seem remarkable to Blake. He had quarreled with his wife, but so did every other man born of woman. It was human nature. In any place where you can hear their voices—a hotel courtyard, an air shaft, a street on a summer evening—you will hear harsh words.

The hard feeling between Blake and Mr. Watkins also had to do with Blake's family, but it was not as serious or as troublesome as what lay behind Mrs. Compton's fleeting smile. The Watkinses rented. Mr. Watkins broke the sumptuary laws day after day—he once went to the eight-fourteen in a pair of sandals—and he made his living as a commercial artist. Blake's oldest son—Charlie was fourteen—had made friends with the Watkins boy. He had spent a lot of time in the sloppy rented house where the Watkinses lived. The friendship had affected his manners and his neatness. Then he had begun to take some meals with the Watkinses, and to spend Saturday nights there. When he had moved most of his possessions over to the Watkinses' and had begun to spend more than half his nights there, Blake had been forced to act. He had spoken not to Charlie but to Mr. Watkins, and had, of necessity, said a number of things that must have sounded critical. Mr. Watkins' long and dirty hair and his corduroy jacket reassured Blake that he had been in the right.

But Mrs. Compton's dying smile and Mr. Watkins' dirty hair did not lessen the pleasure Blake took in settling himself in an uncomfortable seat on the five-forty-eight deep underground. The coach was old and smelled oddly like a bomb shelter in which whole families had spent the night. The light that spread from the ceiling down onto their heads and shoulders was dim. The filth on the window glass was streaked with rain from some other journey, and clouds of rank pipe and cigarette smoke had begun to rise from behind each newspaper, but it was a scene that meant to Blake that he was on a safe path, and after his brush with danger he even felt a little warmth toward Mrs. Compton and Mr. Watkins.

The train traveled up from underground into the weak daylight, and the slums and the city reminded Blake vaguely of the woman who had followed him. To avoid speculation or remorse about her, he turned his attention to the evening paper. Out of the corner of his eye he could see the landscape. It was industrial and, at that hour, sad. There were machine sheds and warehouses, and above these he saw a break in the clouds—a piece of yellow light. "Mr. Blake," someone said. He looked up. It was she. She was standing there holding one hand on the back of the seat to steady herself in the swaying coach. He remembered her name then—Miss Dent. "Hello, Miss Dent," he said.

"Do you mind if I sit here?"

"I guess not."

"Thank you. It's very kind of you. I don't like to inconvenience you like this. I don't want to . . ." He had been frightened when he looked up and saw her, but her timid voice rapidly reassured him. He shifted his hams—that futile and reflexive gesture of hospitality—and she sat down. She sighed. He smelled her wet clothing. She wore a formless black hat with a cheap crest stitched onto it. Her coat was thin cloth, he saw, and she wore gloves and carried a large pocketbook.

"Are you living out in this direction now, Miss Dent?"

"No."

She opened her purse and reached for her handkerchief. She had begun to cry. He turned his head to see if anyone in the car was looking, but no one was. He had sat beside a thousand passengers on the evening train. He had noticed their clothes, the holes in their gloves; and if they fell asleep and mumbled he had wondered what their worries were. He had classified almost all of them briefly before he buried his nose in the paper. He had marked them as rich, poor, brilliant or dull, neighbors or strangers, but no one of the thousands had ever wept. When she opened her purse, he remembered her perfume. It had clung to his skin the night he went to her place for a drink.

"I've been very sick," she said. "This is the first time I've been out of bed in two weeks. I've been terribly sick."

"I'm sorry that you've been sick, Miss Dent," he said in a voice loud enough to be heard by Mr. Watkins and Mrs. Compton. "Where are you working now?"

"What?"

"Where are you working now?"

"Oh, don't make me laugh," she said softly.

"I don't understand."

"You poisoned their minds."

He straightened his back and braced his shoulders. These wrenching movements expressed a brief—and hopeless—longing to be in some other place. She meant trouble. He took a breath. He looked with deep feeling at the half-filled, half-lighted coach to affirm his sense of actuality, of a world in which there was not very much bad trouble after all. He was conscious of her heavy breathing and the smell of her rain-soaked coat. The train stopped. A nun and a man in overalls got off. When it started again, Blake put on his hat and reached for his raincoat.

"Where are you going?" she said.

"I'm going up to the next car."

"Oh, no," she said. "No, no, no." She put her white face so close to his ear that he could feel her warm breath on his cheek. "Don't do that," she whispered. "Don't try and escape me. I have a pistol and I'll have to kill you and I don't want to. All I want to do is to talk with you. Don't move or I'll kill you. Don't, don't, don't!"

Blake sat back abruptly in his seat. If he had wanted to stand and shout for help, he would not have been able to. His tongue had swelled to twice its size, and when he tried to move it, it stuck horribly to the roof of his mouth. His legs were limp. All he could think of to do then was to wait for his heart to stop its hysterical beating, so that he could judge the extent of his danger. She was sitting a little sidewise, and in her pocketbook was the pistol, aimed at his belly.

"You understand me now, don't you?" she said. "You understand that I'm serious?" He tried to speak but he was still mute. He nodded his head. "Now we'll sit quietly for a little while," she said. "I got so excited that my thoughts are all confused. We'll sit quietly for a little while, until I can get my thoughts in order again."

Help would come, Blake thought. It was only a question of minutes. Someone, noticing the look on his face or her peculiar posture, would stop and interfere, and it would all be over. All he had to do was to wait until someone noticed his predicament. Out of the window he saw the river and the sky. The rain clouds were rolling down like a shutter, and while he watched, a streak of orange light on the horizon became brilliant. Its brilliance spread—he could see it move —across the waves until it raked the banks of the river with a dim firelight. Then it was put out. Help would come in a minute, he thought. Help would come before they stopped again; but the train stopped, there were some comings and goings, and Blake still lived on, at the mercy of the woman beside him. The possibility that help might not come was one that he could not face. The possibility that his predicament was not noticeable, that Mrs. Compton would guess that he was taking a poor relation out to dinner at Shady Hill, was something he would think about later. Then the saliva came back into his mouth and he was able to speak.

"Miss Dent?"

"Yes."

"What do you want?"

"I want to talk with you."

"You can come to my office."

"Oh, no. I went there every day for two weeks."

"You could make an appointment."

"No," she said. "I think we can talk here. I wrote you a letter but I've been too sick to go out and mail it. I've put down all my thoughts. I like to travel. I like trains. One of my troubles has always been that I could never afford to travel. I suppose you see this scenery every night and don't notice it any more, but it's nice for someone who's been in bed a long time. They say that He's not in the river and the hills but I think He is. 'Where shall wisdom be found,' it says. 'Where is the place of understanding? The depth saith it is not in me; the sea saith it is not with me. Destruction and death say we have heard the force with our ears.'

"Oh, I know what you're thinking," she said. "You're thinking that I'm crazy, and I have been very sick again but I'm going to be better. It's going to make me better to talk with you. I was in the hospital all the time before I came to work for you but they never tried to cure me, they only wanted to take away my self-respect. I haven't had any work now for three months. Even if I did have to kill you, they wouldn't be able to do anything to me except put me back in the hospital, so you see I'm not afraid. But let's sit quietly for a little while longer. I have to be calm."

The train continued its halting progress up the bank of the river, and Blake tried to force himself to make some plans for escape, but the immediate threat to his life made this difficult, and instead of planning sensibly, he thought of the many ways in which he could have avoided her in the first place. As soon as he had felt these regrets, he realized their futility. It was like regretting his lack of suspicion when she

127

first mentioned her months in the hospital. It was like regretting his failure to have been warned by her shyness, her diffidence, and the handwriting that looked like the marks of a claw. There was no way now of rectifying his mistakes, and he felt—for perhaps the first time in his mature life—the full force of regret. Out of the window, he saw some men fishing on the nearly dark river, and then a ramshackle boat club that seemed to have been nailed together out of scraps of wood that had been washed up on the shore.

Mr. Watkins had fallen asleep. He was snoring. Mrs. Compton read her paper. The train creaked, slowed, and halted infirmly at another station. Blake could see the southbound platform, where a few passengers were waiting to go into the city. There was a workman with a lunch pail, a dressed-up woman, and a man with a suitcase. They stood apart from one another. Some advertisements were posted on the wall behind them. There was a picture of a couple drinking a toast in wine, a picture of a Cat's Paw rubber heel, and a picture of a Hawaiian dancer. Their cheerful intent seemed to go no farther than the puddles of water on the platform and to expire there. The platform and the people on it looked lonely. The train drew away from the station into the scattered lights of a slum and then into the darkness of the country and the river.

"I want you to read my letter before we get to Shady Hill," she said. "It's on the seat. Pick it up. I would have mailed it to you, but I've been too sick to go out. I haven't gone out for two weeks. I haven't had any work for three months. I haven't spoken to anybody but the landlady. Please read my letter."

He picked up the letter from the seat where she had put it. The cheap paper felt abhorrent and filthy to his fingers. It was folded and refolded. "Dear Husband," she had written, in that crazy, wandering hand, "they say that human love leads us to divine love, but is this true? I dream about you every night. I have such terrible desires. I have always had a gift for dreams. I dreamed on Tuesday of a volcano erupting with blood. When I was in the hospital they said they wanted to cure me but they only wanted to take away my self-respect. They only wanted me to dream about sewing and basketwork but I protected my gift for dreams. I'm clair-voyant. I can tell when the telephone is going to ring. I've never had a true friend in my whole life. . . ."

The train stopped again. There was another platform, another picture of the couple drinking a toast, the rubber heel, and the Hawaiian dancer. Suddenly she pressed her face close to Blake's again and whispered in his ear. "I know what you're thinking. I can see it in your face. You're thinking you can get away from me in Shady Hill, aren't you? Oh, I've been planning this for weeks. It's all I've had to think about. I won't harm you if you'll let me talk. I've been thinking about devils. I mean if there are devils in the world, if there are people in the world who represent evil, is it our duty to exterminate them? I know that you always prey on weak people. I can tell. Oh, sometimes I think that I ought to kill you. Sometimes I think you're the only obstacle between me and my happiness. Sometimes . . ."

She touched Blake with the pistol. He felt the muzzle against his belly. The bullet, at that distance, would make a small hole where it entered, but it would rip out of his

129

back a place as big as a soccer ball. He remembered the
unburied dead he had seen in the war. The memory came in
a rush: entrails, eyes, shattered bone, ordure, and other filth.

"All I've ever wanted in life is a little love," she said. She
lightened the pressure of the gun. Mr. Watkins still slept.
Mrs. Compton was sitting calmly with her hands folded in
her lap. The coach rocked gently, and the coats and mush-
room-colored raincoats that hung between the windows
swayed a little as the car moved. Blake's elbow was on the
window sill and his left shoe was on the guard above the
steampipe. The car smelled like some dismal classroom.
The passengers seemed asleep and apart, and Blake felt that
he might never escape the smell of heat and wet clothing
and the dimness of the light. He tried to summon the calcu-
lated self-deceptions with which he sometimes cheered himself, but he was left without any energy for hope or self-
deception.

The conductor put his head in the door and said "Shady
Hill, next, Shady Hill."

"Now," she said. "Now you get out ahead of me."

Mr. Watkins waked suddenly, put on his coat and hat, and
smiled at Mrs. Compton, who was gathering her parcels to
her in a series of maternal gestures. They went to the door.
Blake joined them, but neither of them spoke to him or
seemed to notice the woman at his back. The conductor
threw open the door, and Blake saw on the platform of the
next car a few other neighbors who had missed the express,
waiting patiently and tiredly in the wan light for their trip
to end. He raised his head to see through the open door the
abandoned mansion outside of town, a NO TRESPASSING sign

nailed to a tree, and then the oil tanks. The concrete abutments of the bridge passed, so close to the open door that he could have touched them. Then he saw the first of the lampposts on the northbound platform, the sign SHADY HILL in black and gold, and the little lawn and flower bed kept up by the Improvement Association, and then the cab stand and a corner of the old-fashioned depot. It was raining again; it was pouring. He could hear the splash of water and see the lights reflected in puddles and in the shining pavement, and the idle sound of splashing and dripping formed in his mind a conception of shelter, so light and strange that it seemed to belong to a time of his life that he could not remember.

He went down the steps with her at his back. A dozen or so cars were waiting by the station with their motors running. A few people got off from each of the other coaches; he recognized most of them, but none of them offered to give him a ride. They walked separately or in pairs—purposefully out of the rain to the shelter of the platform, where the car horns called to them. It was time to go home, time for a drink, time for love, time for supper, and he could see the lights on the hill—lights by which children were being bathed, meat cooked, dishes washed—shining in the rain. One by one, the cars picked up the heads of families, until there were only four left. Two of the stranded passengers drove off in the only taxi the village had. "I'm sorry, darling," a woman said tenderly to her husband when she drove up a few minutes later. "All our clocks are slow." The last man looked at his watch, looked at the rain, and then walked off into it, and Blake saw him go as if they had some reason to

131

say good-by—not as we say good-by to friends after a party but as we say good-by when we are faced with an inexorable and unwanted parting of the spirit and the heart. The man's footsteps sounded as he crossed the parking lot to the sidewalk, and then they were lost. In the station, a telephone began to ring. The ringing was loud, plaintive, evenly spaced, and unanswered. Someone wanted to know about the next train to Albany, but Mr. Flanagan, the stationmaster, had gone home an hour ago. He had turned on all his lights before he went away. They burned in the empty waiting room. They burned, tin-shaded, at intervals up and down the platform and with the peculiar sadness of dim and purposeless light. They lighted the Hawaiian dancer, the couple drinking a toast, the rubber heel.

"I've never been here before," she said. "I thought it would look different. I didn't think it would look so shabby. Let's get out of the light. Go over there."

His legs felt sore. All his strength was gone. "Go on," she said.

North of the station there were a freight house and a coalyard and an inlet where the butcher and the baker and the man who ran the service station moored the dinghies from which they fished on Sundays, sunk now to the gunwales with the rain. As he walked toward the freight house, he saw a movement on the ground and heard a scraping sound, and then he saw a rat take its head out of a paper bag and regard him. The rat seized the bag in its teeth and dragged it into a culvert.

"Stop," she said. "Turn around. Oh, I ought to feel sorry for you. Look at your poor face. But you don't know what

I've been through. I'm afraid to go out in the daylight. I'm afraid the blue sky will fall down on me. I'm like poor Chicken-Licken. I only feel like myself when it begins to get dark. But still and all I'm better than you. I still have good dreams sometimes. I dream about picnics and Heaven and the brotherhood of man, and about castles in the moonlight and a river with willow trees all along the edge of it and foreign cities, and after all I know more about love than you."

He heard from off the dark river the the drone of an outboard motor, a sound that drew slowly behind it across the dark water such a burden of clear, sweet memories of gone summers and gone pleasures that it made his flesh crawl, and he thought of dark in the mountains and the children singing. "They never wanted to cure me," she said. "They . . ." The noise of a train coming down from the north drowned out her voice, but she went on talking. The noise filled his ears, and the windows where people ate, drank, slept, and read flew past. When the train had passed beyond the bridge, the noise grew distant, and he heard her screaming at him, "*Kneel down!* Kneel down! Do what I say. *Kneel down!*"

He got to his knees. He bent his head. "There," she said. "You see, if you do what I say, I won't harm you, because I really don't want to harm you, I want to help you, but when I see your face it sometimes seems to me that I can't help you. Sometimes it seems to me that if I were good and loving and sane—oh, much better than I am—sometimes it seems to me that if I were all these things and young and beautiful, too, and if I called to show you the right way, you wouldn't heed me. Oh, I'm better than you, I'm better than you, and

I shouldn't waste my time or spoil my life like this. Put your face in the dirt. *Put your face in the dirt!* Do what I say. Put your face in the dirt."

He fell forward in the filth. The coal skinned his face. He stretched out on the ground, weeping. "Now I feel better," she said. "Now I can wash my hands of you, I can wash my hands of all this, because you see there is some kindness, some saneness in me that I can find again and use. I can wash my hands." Then he heard her footsteps go away from him, over the rubble. He heard the clearer and more distant sound they made on the hard surface of the platform. He heard them diminish. He raised his head. He saw her climb the stairs of the wooden footbridge and cross it and go down to the other platform, where her figure in the dim light looked small, common, and harmless. He raised himself out of the dust—warily at first, until he saw by her attitude, her looks, that she had forgotten him; that she had completed what she had wanted to do, and that he was safe. He got to his feet and picked up his hat from the ground where it had fallen and walked home.

JUST TELL ME WHO IT WAS

✳ **WILL PYM** was a self-made man; that is, he had started his adult life without a nickel or a connection, other than the general friendliness of man to man, and had risen to a vice-presidency in a rayon-blanket firm. He made a large annual contribution to the Baltimore settlement house that had set his feet upon the right path, and he had a few anecdotes to tell about working as a farmhand long, long ago, but his appearance and demeanor were those of a well-established member of the upper middle class, with hardly a trace—hardly a trace of the anxieties of a man who has been through a grueling struggle to put some money into the bank. It is true that beggars, old men in rags, thinly dressed men and women eating bad food in the penitential lights of a cafeteria, slums and squalid mill towns, the faces in rooming-house windows—even a hole in his daughter's socks—could remind him of his youth and make him uneasy. He did not ever like to see the signs of poverty. He took a deep pleasure in the Dutch Colonial house where he lived—in its many lighted windows, in the soundness of his roof and his heating plant—in the warmth of his children's clothing, and

137

in the fact that he had been able to make something plausible and coherent in spite of his mean beginnings. He was always conscious and sometimes mildly resentful of the fact that most of his business associates and all of his friends and neighbors had been skylarking on the turf at Groton or Deerfield or some such school while he was taking books on how to improve your grammar and vocabulary out of the public library. But he recognized this dim resentment of people whose development had been along easier lines than his own as some meanness in his character. Considering merely his physical bulk, it was astonishing that he should have preserved an image of himself as a hungry youth standing outside a lighted window in the rain. He was a cheerful, heavy man with a round face that looked exactly like a pudding. Everyone was glad to see him, as one is glad to see, at the end of a meal, the appearance of a bland, fragrant, and nourishing dish made of fresh eggs, nutmeg, and country cream.

Will had not married until he was past forty and had moved to New York. He had not had the money or the time, and the destitution of his youth had not been sweetened by much natural love. His stepmother—wearing a nightgown for comfort and a flowered hat for looks—had spent her days sitting in their parlor window in Baltimore drinking sherry out of a coffee cup. She was not a jolly old toper, and what she had to say was usually bitter. The picture she presented may have left with Will some skepticism about the emotional richness of human involvements. It may have delayed his marriage. When he finally did marry, he picked a woman much younger than he—a sweet-tempered girl with red hair and green eyes. She sometimes called him Daddy.

Will was so proud of her and spoke so extravagantly of her beauty and her wit that when people first met her they were always disappointed. But Will had been poor and cold and alone, and when he came home at the end of the day to a lovely and loving woman, when he took off his hat and coat in the front hall, he would literally groan with joy. Every stick of furniture that Maria bought seemed to him to be hallowed by her taste and charm. A footstool or a set of pots would so delight him that he would cover her face and throat with kisses. She was extravagant, but he seemed to want a childish and capricious wife, and the implausible excuses that she made for having bought something needless and expensive aroused in him the deepest tenderness. Maria was not much of a cook, but when she put a plate of canned soup in front of him on the maid's night out, he would get up from his end of the table and embrace her with gratitude.

At first, they had a big apartment in the East Seventies. They went out a good deal. Will disliked parties, but he concealed this distaste for the sake of his young wife. At dinners, he would look across the table at her in the candlelight— laughing, talking, and flashing the rings he had bought her— and sigh deeply. He was always impatient for the party to end, so that they would be alone again, in a taxi or in an empty street where he could kiss her. When Maria first got pregnant, he couldn't describe his happiness. Every development in her condition astonished him. He was captivated by the preparations she made for the baby. When their first child was born, when milk flowed from her breasts, when their daughter excited in her a most natural tenderness, he was amazed.

The Pyms had three girls. When their third child was born,

they moved to the suburbs. Will was past fifty then, but he carried Maria over the threshold, lighted a fire in the hearth, and observed all kinds of sentimental and amorous rites in taking possession of the house. To tell the truth, he did seem, once in a while, to talk about Maria too much. He was anxious to have her shine. At parties, he would stop the general conversation and announce, "Maria will now tell us something very funny that happened at the Woman's Club this afternoon." Riding into town on the commuting train, he would ring in her opinions on the baseball season or the excise tax. Eating dinner alone in a hotel in Rochester or Toledo—for he often traveled on business—he would show the waitress a picture of Maria. When he served on the grand jury, all the other members of the panel knew about Maria long before the session ended. When he went salmon fishing in Newfoundland, he wondered constantly if Maria was all right.

On a Saturday in the early spring, they celebrated their tenth wedding anniversary with a party at their house in Shady Hill. Twenty-five or thirty people came to drink their health in champagne. Most of the guests were Maria's age. Will did not like her to be surrounded by young men, and he supervised her comings and goings with a nearly paternal scrutiny. When she wandered out onto the terrace, he was not far behind. But he was a good host, and he held in admirable equilibrium the pleasure he took in his guests and the pleasure he took in thinking that they soon would all be gone. He watched Maria talking with Henry Bulstrode across the room. He supposed that ten years of marriage must have left lines on her face and wasted her figure, but he could see only that her beauty had improved. A pretty young

140

woman was talking with him, but his admiration of Maria made him absent-minded. "You must get Maria to tell you what happened at the florist's this morning," he said.

Late on Sunday afternoon, the Pyms took a walk with their children, as they usually did when the weather was fair. It was that time of year when the woods are still bleak, and mixed with the smells of rotted and changing things is an unaccountable sweetness—a perfume as heavy as roses— although nothing is in flower. The children went on ahead. Will and Maria walked arm in arm. It was nearly dusk. Crows were calling hoarsely to one another in some tall pines. It was that hour of a spring day—or evening—when the dark of the woods and the cold and damp from any nearby pond or brook are suddenly felt, when you realize that the world was lighted, until a minute ago, merely by the sun's fire, and that your clothes are thin.

Will stopped and took a knife from his pocket and began to cut their initials in the bark of a tree. What sense would there be in pointing out that his hair was thin? He meant to express love. It was Maria's youth and beauty that had informed his senses and left his mind so open that the earth seemed spread out before his eyes like a broad map of reason and sensuality. It was her company that made the singing of the crows so fine to hear. For his children, whose voices sounded down the path, he held out the most practical and abundant hopes. All that he had ever been deprived of was now his.

But Maria was cold and tired and hungry. They had not gone to bed until two, and it had been an effort for her to keep her eyes open while they walked in the woods. When

141

they got home, she would have to fix the supper. Cold cuts or lamb chops, she wondered while she watched Will enclose their initials in the outline of a heart and pierce it with an arrow. "Oh, you're so lovely!" she heard him murmur when he had finished. "You're so young and beautiful!" He groaned; he took her in his arms and kissed her wildly. She went on worrying about the supper.

On a Monday night not long after this, Maria sat in the living room tying paper apple blossoms to branches. She was on the committee in charge of decorations for the Apple Blossom Fete, a costume ball given for charity at the country club each year. Will was reading a magazine while he waited for her to finish her work. He wore bedroom slippers and a red brocade smoking jacket—a present from Maria—which bunched in thick folds around his stomach, making him look portly. Maria's hands moved quickly. When she had covered a branch with blossoms, she would hold it up and say, "Isn't that pretty?" Then she would stand it in a corner where there was the beginning of a forest of flowering branches. Upstairs, the three children slept.

The decorations-committee job was the kind of thing Maria did best. She did not like to go to early-morning meetings on the reform of the primary system, or to poke her nose into dirty hospital kitchens, or to meet with other women in the late afternoons to discuss trends in modern fiction. She had tried being secretary of the Woman's Club, but her minutes were so garbled that she had had to be replaced—not without some hard feeling. On the evening of the day when she was relieved of her position, Will had found her in tears, and it had taken him hours to console her. He relished these adversities. She was young and beautiful, and anything that turned her to him for succor only made his position more secure. Later, when Maria was put in charge of the mink-stole raffle to raise some money for the hospital, she had kept such poor records that Will had had to stay home from the office for a day to straighten things out. She cried and he comforted her, where a younger husband might have expressed some impatience. Will did not encourage her inefficiency, but it was a trait that he associated with the fineness of her eyes and her pallor.

While she tied flowers she talked about the fete. There was going to be a twelve-piece orchestra. The decorations had never been so beautiful. They hoped to raise ten thousand dollars. The dressmaker had delivered her costume. Will asked what her costume was, and she said she would go upstairs and put it on. She usually went to the Apple Blossom Fete as a figure from French history, and Will's interest was not intense.

Half an hour later, she came down, and went to the mirror by the piano. She was wearing gold slippers, pink tights, and a light velvet bodice, cut low enough to show the division of her breasts. "Of course, my hair will be all different," she said. "And I haven't decided what jewels to wear."

A terrible sadness came over Will. The tight costume—he had to polish his eyeglasses to see it better—displayed all the beauty he worshiped, and it also expressed her perfect innocence of the wickedness of the world. The sight filled poor Will with lust and dismay. He couldn't bear to disappoint her, and yet he couldn't let her flagrantly provoke his

143

neighbors—a group of men who seemed at that moment, to his unsettled mind, to be voracious, youthful, bestial, and lewd. Watching her pose happily in front of the mirror, he thought that she looked like a child—a maiden, at least—approaching some obscene doom. In her sweet and gentle face and her half-naked bosom he saw all the sadness of life.

"You can't wear that, Mummy," he said.

"What?" She turned away from the mirror.

"Mummy, you'll get pinched to death."

"Everybody else is going to wear tights, Willy. Helen Benson and Grace Heatherstone are going to wear tights."

"They're different, Mummy," he said sadly. "They're very different. They're tough, hardheaded, cynical, worldly women."

"What am I?"

"You're lovely and you're innocent," he said. "You don't understand what a bunch of dogs men are."

"I don't want to be lovely and innocent all the time."

"Oh, Mummy, you don't mean that! You can't mean that! You don't know what you're saying."

"I only want to have a good time."

"Don't you have a good time with me?"

She began to cry. She threw herself on the sofa and buried her face. Her tears ate like acid into Will's resolve as he bent over her slender and miserable form. Years and years ago he had wondered if a young wife would give him trouble. Now, with his eyeglasses steaming and the brocade jacket bunched up around his stomach, he stood face to face with the problem. How—even when they were in grave danger —could he refuse innocence and beauty? "All right, Mummy,

144

all right," he said. He was nearly in tears himself. "You can wear it."

Will left the next morning for a trip that took him to Cleveland, Chicago, and Topeka. He called Maria on Tuesday and Wednesday nights, and the maid said that she was out. She would be putting up the decorations in the club, he realized. The pancakes he ate for breakfast on Thursday disagreed with him at once, and gave him a stomach-ache that none of the many medicines he carried with him in his suitcase could cure. Friday was foggy in Kansas, and his plane was grounded until late that night. At the airport, he ate some chicken pie; it made him feel worse. He arrived in New York on Saturday morning, had to go directly to his office, and did not get out to Shady Hill until late Saturday afternoon. It was the day of the party, and Maria was still at the club. He spent an hour raking dead leaves from the flower beds at the side of the house. When Maria came home, he thought she looked superb. Her color was high and her eyes were bright.

She showed Will the costume she had rented for him. It was a suit of chain mail with a helmet. Will was pleased with the costume, because it was a disguise. Exhausted and bilious, he felt he needed a disguise for the dance. When he had bathed and shaved, Maria helped him strap himself into his coat of mail. She cut some ostrich plumes off an old hat and stuck them gaily into his helmet. Will went toward a mirror to see himself, but just as he got there, the visor slammed shut, and he couldn't get it to stay open. He went downstairs, holding on to the banister—the chain mail was heavy—and wedged the visor open with a folded timetable and sat down to have a drink. When Maria came down in her pink tights and her gold slippers, Will rose to admire her. She said that she would not be able to leave the dance early, because she was on the committee; if Will wanted to go home, she would get a ride with someone else. He had never gone home from a party without her, and he hated the idea. Maria put on a wrap and kissed the children, and they went off to dinner at the Beardens'.

At the Beardens', the party was large and late. They drank cocktails until after nine. When they went in to dinner, Will sat beside Ethel Worden. She was a pretty young woman, but she had been drinking Martinis for two hours; her face was drawn and her eyes were red. She said that she loved Will, that she always had, but Will was looking down the table at Maria. Even at that distance, he seemed to take in something vital from the play of shadow upon her face. He would have liked to be near enough to hear what she was saying.

Ethel Worden didn't make it any easier. "We're poor, Will," she said sadly. "Did you know that we're poor? Nobody realizes that there are people like us in a community like this. We can't afford eggs for breakfast. We can't afford a cleaning woman. We can't afford a washing machine. We can't afford . . ."

Before dessert was finished, several couples got up to leave for the club. Will saw Trace Bearden handing Maria her wrap, and got up suddenly. He wanted to get to the club in time to have the first dance with her. When he got outside, Trace and Maria had gone. He asked Ethel Worden to drive over with him. She was delighted. As he put the car in the parking lot at the country club, Ethel began to cry. She was poor and lonely and hungry for love. She drew Will to her and wept on his chain-mail shoulder, while he looked out the back windows of the station wagon to see if he could recognize Trace Bearden's car. He wondered if Maria was already in the clubhouse or if she was having trouble in a parked car herself. He dried Ethel's tears and spoke to her tenderly, and they went in.

It was late by then—it was after midnight—and that dance was always a rhubarb. The floor was crowded, and plumes, crowns, animal heads, and turbans were rocking in the dim light. It was that hour when the band accelerates its beat, when the drums deepen, when the aging dancers utter loud cries of lust and joy, seize their partners by the girdle, and break into all kinds of youthful and wanton specialties— the shimmy, the Charleston, hops, and belly dances. Will danced clumsily in his mail. Now and then, he glimpsed Maria in the distance, but he was never able to catch up with her. Going into the bar for a drink, he saw her at the other end of the room, but the crowd was too dense for him to get to her. She was surrounded by men. He looked for her in the lounge during the next intermission, but he could not find her. When the music started again, he gave the band ten dollars and asked them to play "I Could Write a Book." It was their music. She would hear it through the bedlam. It would remind her of their marriage, and she would leave her partner and find him. He waited alone at the edge of the floor through this song.

Discouraged, then, and tired from his traveling and the

weight of his chain mail, he went into the lounge, took off his helmet, and fell asleep. When he woke, a half hour later, he saw Larry Helmsford taking Ethel Worden out the terrace door toward the parking lot. She was staggering. Will wandered back to the ballroom, drawn there by shouts of excitement. Someone had set fire to a feathered headdress. The fire was being put out with champagne. It was after three o'clock. Will put on his helmet, propped the visor open with a folded match paper, and went home.

Maria danced the last dance. She had a drink from the last bottle of wine. It was morning then. The band had gone, but a pianist was still playing and a few couples were dancing in the daylight. Breakfast parties were forming, but she refused these invitations in order to drive home with the Beardens. Will might be worried. After she said good-by to the Beardens, she stood on her front steps to get some air. She had lost her pocketbook. Her tights had been torn by the scales of a dragon. The smell of spilled wine came from her clothes. The sweetness of the air and the fineness of the light touched her. The party seemed like gibberish. She had had all the partners she wanted, but she had not had all the right ones. The hundreds of apple blossoms that she had tied to branches and that had looked, at a distance, so like real blossoms would soon be swept into the ash can.

The trees of Shady Hill were filled with birds—larks, thrushes, robins, crows—and now the air began to ring with their song. The pristine light and the loud singing reminded her of some ideal—some simple way of life, in which she dried her hands on an apron and Will came home from the sea—that she had betrayed. She did not know where she had

148

failed, but the gentle morning light illuminated her failure pitilessly. She began to cry.

Will was asleep, but he woke when she opened the front door. "Mummy?" he asked as she climbed the stairs. "Mummy? . . . Hello, Mummy. Good morning!" She didn't reply.

He saw her tears, the gash in her tights and the stains on her front. She sat down at her dressing table, laid her face on the glass, and went on crying. "Oh, don't cry, Mummy!" he said. "Don't cry! I don't care, Mummy. I thought I would but I guess it doesn't really matter. I won't ever mention it, Mummy. Now, come to bed. Come to bed and get some sleep."

Her sobbing got louder. He got up and went to the dressing table and put his arms around her. "I told you what would happen if you wore that costume, didn't I? But it doesn't matter any more. I'll never ask you anything about it. I'll forget the whole thing. But come to bed now and get some sleep."

Her head was swimming, and his voice droned on and on, shutting out the noises of the morning. Then his anxious love, his nagging passion, were more than she could support. "I don't care. I'm willing to forget it," he said.

She got out of his embrace, crossed the room to the hall, and shut the guest-room door in his face.

Downstairs, sitting over a cup of coffee, Will realized that his supervision of Maria's life had been anything but thorough. If she had wanted to deceive him, her life couldn't have been planned along more convenient lines. In the summer, she was alone most of the time, except weekends. He was away on business one week out of every month. She went to New York whenever she pleased—sometimes in the evening. Only a week before the dance she had gone into town to have dinner with some old friends. She had planned to come home on a train that reached Shady Hill at eleven. Will drove to the station to meet her. It was a rainy night and he remembered waiting, in a rather gloomy frame of mind, on the station platform. As soon as he saw the distant lights of the train, his mood was changed by the anticipation of greeting her and taking her home. When the train stopped and only Charlie Curtin—half tipsy—got off, Will was disappointed and worried. Soon after he got home, the telephone rang. It was Maria calling to say that she had missed the train and would not be home until two. At two, Will returned to the station. It was still rainy. Maria and Henry Bulstrode were the only passengers. She walked swiftly up the platform in the rain to kiss Will. He remembered that there had been tears in her eyes, but he had not thought anything about it at the time. Now he wondered about her tears.

A few nights before that, she had said, after dinner, that she wanted to go to the movies in the village. Will had offered to take her, although he was tired, but she said she knew how much he disliked movies. It had seemed odd to him at the time that before going off to the nine-o'clock show she should take a bath, and when she came downstairs, he heard, under her mink coat, the rustling of a silk dress. He fell asleep before she returned, and for all he knew, she might have come in at dawn. It had always seemed generous of her not to insist on his going with her to meetings of the Civic Improvement Association, but how did he know whether she had gone off to discuss the fluorination of water or to meet a lover?

He remembered something that had happened in February. The Woman's Club had given a revue for charity. He had known before he went to it that Maria was going to do a dance expressing the view of the Current Events Committee on the tariff. She came onto the stage to the music of "A Pretty Girl Is Like a Melody." She wore a long evening dress, gloves, and a fur piece—the recognizable getup of a strip-tease artist—and, to his dismay, she was given a rousing reception. Maria walked around the stage and took off her fur piece, to applause, shouts, and some whistling. During the next chorus, she peeled off her gloves. Will pretended to be enjoying himself, but he had begun to sweat. With the third chorus, she took off her belt. This was all, but the uproarious applause she had been given rang again in Will's ears now and made them warm.

A few weeks earlier, Will had gone uptown for lunch—a thing he seldom did. Walking down Madison Avenue, he thought he saw Maria ahead of him, with another man. The dark-red suit, the fur piece, and the hat were hers. He did not recognize the man. Acting impulsively where he might have acted stealthily, he had shouted her name—"Maria! Maria! Maria!" The street was crowded, and there was the distance of half a block between them. Before he could reach the woman, she disappeared. She might have stepped into a taxi or a store. That evening, when he said to Maria, cheerfully enough, that he thought he saw her on Madison Avenue, she answered crossly, "Well you didn't." After dinner, she claimed to have a headache. She asked him to sleep in the guest room.

The afternoon of the day after the dance, Will took the children for a walk without Maria. He lectured them, as he always did, on the names of the trees. "That's a ginkgo. . . . That's a weeping beech. . . . That bitter smell comes from the boxwood in the hollow." It may have been because he had received no education himself that he liked to give an educational tone to his time with the children. They recited the states of the Union at the lunch table, discussed geology during some of their walks, and named the stars in the sky if they stayed out after dusk. Will was determined to be cheerful this afternoon, but the figures of his children, walking ahead, saddened him, for they seemed like live symbols of his trouble. He had not actually thought of leaving Maria—he had not let the idea form—but he seemed to breathe the atmosphere of separation. When he passed the tree where he had carved their initials, he thought of the stupendous wickedness of the world.

The house was dark when they came back up the driveway at the end of their walk—dark and cold. Will turned on some lights and heated the coffee he had made at breakfast. The telephone rang, but he did not answer it. He took a cup of coffee up to the guest room, where Maria was. He thought at first that she was still sleeping. When he turned on the light, he saw that she was sitting against the pillows. She smiled, but he responded warily to her charm.

"Here's some coffee, Mummy."

"Thank you. Did you have a nice walk?"

"Yes."

"I feel better," she said. "What time is it?"

"Half past five."

"I don't feel strong enough to go to the Townsends'."

"Then I won't go."

"Oh, I wish you would, Willy. Please go to the party and come home and tell me all about it. Please go."

Now that she urged him, the party seemed like a good idea.

"You must go, Will," Maria said. "There'll be a lot of gossip about the dance, and you can hear it all, and then you can come home and tell me all about it. Please go to the party, darling. It will make me feel guilty if you stay home on my account."

At the Townsends', cars were parked on both sides of the street, and all the windows of the big house were brightly lighted. Will stepped into the lamplight, the firelight, and the cheerful human noises of the gathering with a sincere desire to lose his heaviness of spirit. He went upstairs to leave his coat. Bridget, an old Irishwoman, took it. She was a free-lance maid who worked at most of the big parties in Shady Hill. Her husband was caretaker at the country club. "So your lady isn't with you," she said, in her sweet brogue. "Ah, well, I can't say that I blame her." Then she laughed suddenly. She put her hands on her knees and rocked back and forth. "I shouldn't tell you, I know, so help me God, but when Mike was sweeping up the parking lot this morning, he found a pair of gold slippers and a blue lace girdle."

Downstairs, Will spoke with his hostess, and she said she was so sorry that Maria hadn't come. Crossing the living room, he was stopped by Pete Parsons, who drew him over to the fireplace and told him a joke. This was what Will had come for, and his spirits began to improve. But, going from Pete Parsons toward the door of the bar, he found his way blocked by Biff Worden. Ethel's story of their neediness, her tears, and her trip to the parking lot with Larry Helmsford were still fresh in his mind. He did not want to see Biff Worden. He did not like it that Biff could muster a cheerful and open face after his wife had been seduced in the Helmsfords' station wagon.

"Did you hear what Mike Reilly found in the parking lot this morning?" Biff asked. "A pair of slippers and a girdle." Will said that he wanted a drink, and he got past Biff, but the entrance to the passage between the living room and the bar was blocked by the Chesneys.

In almost every suburb there is a charming young couple designated by their gifts to be an ambassadorial pair. They are the ones who meet John Mason Brown at the train and drive him to the auditorium. They are the ones who organize the bumper tennis tournaments, handle the most difficult cases in the fund-raising campaign, and can be counted on by their hostesses to humor the bore, pass the stuffed celery, breathe fire into the dying conversation, and expel the drunk. Their social and family connections are indescribably rich and varied, and physically they are models of attractiveness and fashion—direct, mild, well groomed, their eyes twinkling with trust and friendliness. Such a young couple were the Chesneys.

"So glad to see you," Mark Chesney said, removing his pipe from his mouth and putting a hand on Will's shoulder. "Missed you at the dance last night, although I saw Maria enjoying herself. But what I wanted to speak to you about is something of a higher order. Give me a minute? As you may or may not know, I'm in charge of the adult-education program at the high school this year. We've had a disappointing attendance, and we have a speaker coming on Thursday for whom I'm anxious to rustle up a sizeable audience. Her name is Mary Bickwald, and she's going to speak on marriage problems—extramarital affairs, that sort of thing. If you and Maria are free on Thursday, I think you'll find it worth your time." The Chesneys went on into the living room, and Will continued toward the bar.

The bar was full of a noisy and pleasant company, and Will was glad to join it and get a drink. He had begun to feel like himself when the rector of Christ Church bore down on him, shook his hand, and drew him away from the others.

The rector was a large man and, unlike some of his suburban colleagues, not at all wary of clerical black. When he and Will met at cocktail parties, they usually talked about blankets. Will had given many blankets to the church. He had given blankets to its missions and blankets to its shelters. When the shepherds knelt in the straw at Mary's knees in the Nativity play, they were clothed in Will's blankets. Since he expected to be asked for blankets, he was surprised to hear the rector say, "I want you to feel free to come to my study, Will, and talk to me if anything is troubling you." While Will was thanking the rector for this invitation, they were joined by Herbert McGrath.

Herbert McGrath was a banker, a wealthy, irritable man. At the bottom of his thinking there seemed to be an apprehension—a nightmare—that without the kind of order he represented, the world would fly apart. He despised men who raced to catch the morning train. In the "no-smoking" car, it was customary for people to light cigarettes as the train approached Grand Central Station, and this infringement so irritated Herbert that he would tap his neighbors on the shoulder and tell them that the smoker was in the rear. Mixed with his insistence on propriety was a curious strain of superstition. When he walked along the station platform in the morning, he looked around him. If he saw a coin, he would shoulder his way past the other commuters and bend down to get it. "Good luck, you know," he would explain as he put the coin in his pocket. "You need both luck *and* brains." Now he wanted to talk about the immorality at the party, and Will decided to go home.

He put his glass on the bar and started thoughtfully through the passage to the living room. His head was down, and he walked straight into Mrs. Walpole, a very plain woman. "I see that your wife hasn't recovered sufficiently to face the public today," she said gaily.

A peculiar fate seems to overtake homely women at the ends of parties—and journeys, too. Their curls and their ribbons come undone, particles of food cling to their teeth, their glasses steam, and the wide smile with which they planned to charm the world lapses into a look of habitual discontent and bitterness. Mrs. Walpole had got herself up bravely for the Townsends' party, but time itself—she was drinking sherry—had destroyed the impression she intended to make. Someone seemed to have sat on her hat, her voice was strident, and the camellia pinned to her shoulder had died.

"But I suppose Maria sent you to see what they're saying about her," she said.

Will got past Mrs. Walpole and went up the stairs to get his coat. Bridget had gone, and Helen Bulstrode was sitting alone in the hall in a red dress. Helen was a lush. She was treated kindly in Shady Hill. Her husband was pleasant, wealthy, and forbearing. Now Helen was very drunk, and whatever she had meant to forget when she first poured herself a drink that day had long since been lost in the clutter. She rolled a little in her chair while Will was putting on his coat, and suddenly she addressed him copiously in French. Will did not understand. Her voice got louder and angrier, and when he got down to the hall, she went to the head of the stairs to call after him. He went off without saying good-by to anyone.

Maria was in the living room reading a magazine when Will came in. "Look, Mummy," he said. "Can you tell me this? Did you lose your shoes last night?"

"I lost my pocketbook," Maria said, "but I don't think I lost my shoes."

"Try and remember," he said. "It isn't like a raincoat or an umbrella. People usually remember when they lose their shoes."

"What is the matter with you, Willy?"

"Did you lose your shoes?"

"I don't know."

"Did you wear a girdle?"

"What are you talking about, Will?"

"By Christ, I've got to find out!"

He went upstairs to their room, which was dark. He turned on a light in her closet and opened the chest where she kept her shoes. There were a great many pairs, and among them were gold shoes, silver shoes, bronze shoes, and he was shuffling through the collection when he saw Maria standing in the doorway. "Oh, my God, Mummy, forgive me!" he said. "Forgive me!"

"Oh, Willy!" she exclaimed. "Look what you've done to my shoes."

Will felt all right in the morning, and he had a good day in the city. At five, he made the trip uptown on the subway and crossed the station to his train automatically. In the train, he got an aisle seat and scanned the asininities in the evening paper. An old man was suing his young wife for divorce, on the ground of adultery; the fact that this story had no power to disturb Will not only pleased him but left him feeling exceptionally fit and happy. The train traveled north under a sky that was still spread with light.

A little rain had begun to fall when Will stepped onto the platform at Shady Hill. "Hello, Trace," he said. "Hello, Pete. Hello, Herb." Around him, his neighbors were greeting their wives and children. He took the route up Alewives Lane to Shadrock Road, past rows and rows of lighted houses. He put his car in the garage and went around to the front and looked at his tulips, gleaming in the rain and the porch light. He let the fawning cat in out of the wet, and Flora, his youngest daughter, ran through the hall to kiss him. Some deep recess in his spirit seemed to respond to the good child and the light-filled rooms. He had the feeling that there would never be any less to his life than this. Presently, he would be sitting on a folding chair in the June sunlight watching Flora graduate from Smith.

Maria came into the hall wearing a gray silk dress—a cloth and a color that flattered her. Her eyes were bright and wide, and she kissed him tenderly. The telephone began to ring, for it was that hour in the suburbs when the telephone rings steadily with board-meeting announcements, scraps of gossip, fund-raising pleas, and invitations. Maria answered it and he heard her say "Yes, Edith."

Will went into the living room to make a cocktail, and a few minutes later the doorbell rang. Edith Hastings, a good neighbor and a friendly woman, preceded Maria into the living room, protesting, "I really shouldn't break in on you like this." Still protesting, she sat down and took the glass that Will handed her. He had never seen her color so high or her eyes so bright. "Charlie's in Oregon," she said. "He'll be gone three weeks this trip. He wanted me to speak to you, Will, about some apple trees. He meant to speak to you before he left, but he didn't have the time. He can get apple trees by the dozen from a nursery in New Jersey, and he wanted to know if you wouldn't like to buy six."

Edith Hastings was one of those women—and there were many of them in Shady Hill—whose husbands were away on business from one to three weeks out of every month. They lived—conjugally—the life of a Grand Banks fisherman's wife, with none of the lore of ships and sailors to draw on. None—or almost none—of these widows could be accused of not having attacked their problems gallantly. They solicited funds for cancer, heart trouble, lameness, deafness, and mental health. They cultivated tropical plants in a capricious climate, wove cloth, made pottery, cared tenderly for their children, and did everything else imaginable to make up for the irremediable absence of their men. They remained lonely women with a natural proneness to gossip.

"But of course you don't have to decide this minute," Edith went on when he didn't answer her question. "I don't suppose

159

you really have to decide until Charlie comes back from Oregon. I mean there isn't any special time for planting apple trees, is there? And, speaking of apple trees, how was the fete?"

Will turned his back and opened a window. Outside, the rain fell steadily, but he doubted then that it was the rain that had heightened Edith's color and made her eyes shine. He heard Maria reply, and then he heard Edith ask, "When did you people leave?" She could not keep the excitement out of her voice. "And I understand that a pair of slippers and a girdle—"

Will swung around. "Is that what you came here to talk about?" he asked sharply.

"What?"

"Is that what you came here to talk about?"

"I really came here to talk about apple trees."

"I gave Charlie a check for those apple trees six months ago."

"Charlie didn't tell me."

"Why should he? It was all settled."

"Well, I guess I'd better go."

"Please do," Will said. "Please go. And if anyone asks how we are, tell them we're getting along fine."

"Oh, Will, Will, Will!" Maria said.

"I seem to have come at the wrong time," Edith said.

"And when you call the Trenchers and the Farquarsons and the Abbotts and the Beardens, tell them that I don't give a good God damn what happened at the party. Tell them to think up some gossip about someone else. Tell them to imagine some filth about the Fuller Brush man or the chump who delivers eggs on Friday or the Slaters' gardener, but tell them to leave us alone."

She was gone. Maria, crying, looked at him so wantonly that he nearly choked. Then she climbed the stairs in her gray silk dress and shut the door to their room. He followed her and found her lying on their bed in the dark. "Who was it, Mummy?" he asked. "Just tell me who it was and I'll forget about it."

"It wasn't anybody," she said. "There wasn't anybody."

"Now, Mummy," he said heavily. "I know better than that. I don't want to reproach you. That isn't why I ask. I just want to know so I can forget about it."

"Please let me alone!" she cried. "Please let me alone for a little while."

Waking at dawn in the guest room, Will saw the whole thing clearly. He was astonished to realize how the strength of his feeling had obstructed his vision. The villain was Henry Bulstrode. It was Henry who had been with her on the train when she returned that rainy night at two. It was Henry who had whistled when she did her dance at the Woman's Club. It was Henry's head and shoulders he had seen on Madison Avenue when he recognized Maria ahead of him. And now he remembered poor Helen Bulstrode's haggard face at the Townsends' party—the face of a woman who was married to a libertine. It was her husband's unregeneracy that she had been trying to forget. The spate of drunken French she had aimed at him must have been about Maria and Henry. Henry Bulstrode's face, grinning with naked and lascivious mockery, appeared in the middle of the guest room. There was only one thing to do.

Will bathed, dressed, and ate his breakfast. Maria slept on. It was still early when he finished his coffee, and he decided to walk to the train. He strode down Shadrock Road with the peculiar briskness of the aging. Only a few people had gathered on the platform for the eight-nineteen when he reached the station. Trace Bearden joined him, and then Biff Worden. And then Henry Bulstrode stepped out of the waiting room, showed his white teeth in a smile, and frowned at his newspaper. Without any warning at all, Will walked over to him and knocked him down. Women screamed, and the scuffle that followed was very confusing. Herbert Mc-Grath, who had missed the action, assumed that Henry had started it and stood over him saying, "No more of this, young man! No more of this!" Trace and Biff pinned Will's arms to his sides and quick-stepped him down to the far end of the platform, asking, "You crazy, Will? Have you gone crazy?" Then the eight-nineteen came around the bend, the fracas was suspended by the search for seats, and when the station-master rushed out onto the platform to see what was happening, the train had departed and they were all gone.

The amazing thing was how well Will felt when he boarded the train. Now his fruitful life with Maria would be resumed. They would walk on Sunday afternoons again, and play word games by the open fire again, and weed the roses again, and love one another under the sounds of the rain again, and hear the singing of the crows; and he would buy her a present that afternoon as a signal of love and forgiveness. He would buy her pearls or gold or sapphires—something expensive; emeralds maybe; something no young man could afford.

162

THE TROUBLE OF MARCIE FLINT

✳ "THIS IS being written aboard the S. S. *Augustus,*
three days at sea. My suitcase is full of peanut butter, and I
am a fugitive from the suburbs of all large cities. What holes!
The suburbs, I mean. God preserve me from the camaraderie
of commuting trains, and even from the lovely ladies taking
in their asters and their roses at dusk lest the frost kill them,
and from ladies with their heads whirling with civic zeal. I'm
off to Torino, where the girls love peanut butter and the world
is a man's castle and . . ." There was absolutely nothing wrong
with the suburb (Shady Hill) from which Charles Flint was
fleeing, his age is immaterial, and he was no stranger to
Torino, having been there for three months recently on business.

"God preserve me," he continued, "from women who dress
like *toreros* to go to the supermarket, and from cowhide dis-
patch cases, and from flannels and gabardines. Preserve me
from word games and adulterers, from basset hounds and
swimming pools and frozen canapés and Bloody Marys and
smugness and syringa bushes and P.-T.A. meetings." On
and on he wrote, while the *Augustus,* traveling at seventeen

165

knots, took a course due east; they would raise the Azores in a day.

Like all bitter men, Flint knew less than half the story and was more interested in unloading his own peppery feelings than in learning the truth. Marcie, the wife from whom he was fleeing, was a dark-haired, dark-eyed woman—not young by any stretch of the imagination but gifted with great stores of feminine sweetness and gallantry. She had not told her neighbors that Charlie had left her; she had not even called her lawyer; but she had fired the cook, and she now took a south-southwest course between the stove and the sink, cooking the children's supper. It was not in her to review the past, as her husband would, or to inspect the forces that could put an ocean between a couple who had been cheerfully married for fifteen years. There had been, she felt, a slight difference in their points of view during his recent absence on business, for while he always wrote that he missed her, he also wrote that he was dining at the Superga six nights a week and having a wonderful time. He had only planned to be away for six weeks, and when this stretched out to three months, she found that it was something to be borne.

Her neighbors had stood by her handsomely during the first weeks, but she knew, herself, that an odd woman can spoil a dinner party, and as Flint continued to stay away, she found that she had more and more lonely nights to get through. Now, there were two aspects to the night life of Shady Hill; there were the parties, of course, and then there was another side—a regular Santa Claus's workshop of madrigal singers, political discussion groups, recorder groups, dancing schools, confirmation classes, committee meetings, and

lectures on literature, philosophy, city planning, and pest
control. The bright banner of stars in heaven has probably
never before been stretched above such a picture of nocturnal
industry. Marcie, having a sweet, clear voice, joined a madrigal group that met on Thursdays and a political workshop
that met on Mondays. Once she made herself available, she
was sought as a committeewoman, although it was hard to
say why; she almost never opened her mouth. She finally
accepted a position on the Village Council, in the third month
of Charlie's absence, mostly to keep herself occupied.

Virtuousness, reason, civic zeal, and loneliness all con-
tributed to poor Marcie's trouble. Charlie, far away in Torino,
could imagine her well enough standing in their lighted doorway on the evening of his return, but could he imagine her
groping under the bed for the children's shoes or pouring
bacon fat into an old soup can? "Daddy has to stay in Italy
in order to make the money to buy the things we need," she
told the children. But when Charlie called her from abroad,
as he did once a week, he always seemed to have been drinking. Regard this sweet woman, then, singing "Hodie Christus
Natus Est," studying Karl Marx, and sitting on a hard chair
at meetings of the Village Council.

If there was anything really wrong with Shady Hill, anything that you could put your finger on, it was the fact that
the village had no public library—no foxed copies of Pascal,
smelling of cabbage; no broken sets of Dostoevski and George
Eliot; no Galsworthy, even; no Barrie and no Bennett. This
was the chief concern of the Village Council during Marcie's
term. The library partisans were mostly newcomers to the

167

village; the opposition whip was Mrs. Selfredge, a member of
the Council and a very decorous woman, with blue eyes of
astonishing brilliance and inexpressiveness. Mrs. Selfredge
often spoke of the chosen quietness of their life. "We never
go out," she would say, but in such a way that she seemed
to be expressing not some choice but a deep vein of loneliness.
She was married to a wealthy man much older than herself,
and they had no children; indeed, the most indirect mention
of sexual fact brought a deep color to Mrs. Selfredge's face.
She took the position that a library belonged in that category
of public service that might make Shady Hill attractive to a
development. This was not blind prejudice. Carsen Park, the
next village, had let a development inside its boundaries, with
disastrous results to the people already living there. Their
taxes had been doubled, their schools had been ruined. That
there was any connection between reading and real estate
was disputed by the partisans of the library, until a horrible
murder—three murders, in fact—took place in one of the
cheesebox houses in the Carsen Park development, and the
library project was buried with the victims.

From the terraces of the Superga you can see all of Torino
and the snow-covered mountains around, and a man drinking
wine there might not think of his wife attending a meeting of
the Village Council. This was a board of ten men and two
women, headed by the Mayor, who screened the projects
that came before them. The Council met in the Civic Center,
an old mansion that had been picked up for back taxes. The
board room had been the parlor. Easter eggs had been hidden
here, children had pinned paper tails on paper donkeys, fires
had burned on the hearth, and a Christmas tree had stood in

the corner; but once the house had become the property of the village, a conscientious effort seems to have been made to exorcise these gentle ghosts. Raphael's self-portrait and the pictures of the Broken Bridge at Avignon and the Avon at Stratford were taken down and the walls were painted a depressing shade of green. The fireplace remained, but the flue was sealed up and the bricks were spread with green paint. A track of flourescent tubing across the ceiling threw a withering light down into the faces of the Village Council members and made them all look haggard and tired. The room made Marcie uncomfortable. In its harsh light her sweetness was unavailing, and she felt not only bored but somehow painfully estranged.

On this particular night they discussed water taxes and parking meters, and then the Mayor brought up the public library for the last time. "Of course, the issue is closed," he said, "but we've heard everyone all along, on both sides. There's one more man who wants to speak to us, and I think we ought to hear him. He comes from Maple Dell." Then he opened the door from the board room into the corridor and let Noel Mackham in.

Now, the neighborhood of Maple Dell was more like a development than anything else in Shady Hill. It was the kind of place where the houses stand cheek by jowl, all of them white frame, all of them built twenty years ago, and parked beside each was a car that seemed more substantial than the house itself, as if this were a fragment of some nomadic culture. And it was a kind of spawning ground, a place for bearing and raising the young and for nothing else —for who would ever come back to Maple Dell? Who, in the darkest night, would ever think with longing of the three upstairs bedrooms and the leaky toilet and the sour-smelling halls? Who would ever come back to the little living room where you couldn't swing a cat around without knocking down the colored photograph of Mount Rainier? Who would ever come back to the chair that bit you in the bum and the obsolete TV set and the bent ashtray with its pressed-steel statue of a naked woman doing a scarf dance?

"I understand that the business is closed," Mackham said, "but I just wanted to go on record as being in favor of a public library. It's been on my conscience."

He was not much of an advocate for anything. He was tall. His hair had begun an erratic recession, leaving him with some sparse fluff to comb over his bald brow. His features were angular; his skin was bad. There were no deep notes to his voice. Its range seemed confined to a delicate hoarse-ness—a monotonous and laryngitic sound that aroused in Marcie, as if it had been some kind of Hungarian music, feel-ings of irritable melancholy. "I just wanted to say a few words in favor of a public library," he rasped. "When I was a kid we were poor. There wasn't much good about the way we lived, but there was this Carnegie Library. I started going there when I was about eight. I guess I went there regularly for ten years. I read everything—philosophy, novels, technical books, poetry, ships' logs. I even read a cookbook. For me, this library amounted to the difference between life and death. It meant the difference between success and failure. When I remember the thrill I used to get out of cracking a good book, I just hate to think of bringing my kids up in a place where there isn't any library."

"Well, of course we know what you mean," Mayor Simmons said. "But I don't think that's quite the question. The question is not one of denying books to children. Most of us in Shady Hill have libraries of our own."

Mark Barrett got to his feet. "And *I'd* like to throw in a word about poor boys and reading, if I might," he said, in a voice so full of color and virility that everyone smiled. "I was a poor boy myself," he said cheerfully, "and I'm not ashamed to say so, and I'd just like to throw in—for what it's worth—that I never put my nose inside a public library, except to get out of the rain, or maybe follow a pretty girl. I just don't want anybody to be left with the impression that a public library is the road to success."

"I didn't say that a public library was the road to—"

"Well, you *implied* it!" Barrett shouted, and he seated himself with a big stir. His chair creaked, and by bulging his muscles a little he made his garters, braces, and shoes all sound.

"I only wanted to say—" Mackham began again.

"You *implied* it!" Barrett shouted.

"Just because *you* can't read," Mackham said, "it doesn't follow—"

"Damn it, man, I didn't say that I couldn't read!" Barrett was on his feet again.

"Please, gentlemen! Please! Please!" Mayor Simmons said. "Let's keep our remarks temperate."

"I'm not going to sit here and have someone who lives in Maple Dell tell me the reason he's such a hot rock is because he read a lot of books!" Barrett shouted. "Books have their place. I won't deny it. But no book ever helped me to get

171

where I am, and from where I am I can spit on Maple Dell. As for my kids, I want them out in the fresh air playing ball, not reading cookbooks."

"Please, Mark. Please," the Mayor said. And then he turned to Mrs. Selfredge and asked her to move that the meeting be adjourned.

"My day, my hour, my moment of revelation," Charlie wrote, in his sun-deck cabin on the *Augustus*, "came on a Sunday, when I had been home eight days. Oh God, was I happy! I spent most of the day putting up storm windows, and I like working on my house. Things like putting up storm windows. When the work was done, I put the ladder away and grabbed a towel and my swimming trunks and walked over to the Townsends' swimming pool. They were away, but the pool hadn't been drained. I put on my trunks and dove in and I remember seeing—way, way up in the top of one of the pine trees—a brassière that I guess the Townsend kids had snitched and heaved up there in midsummer, the screams of dismay from their victim having long since been carried away on the west wind. The water was very cold, and blood pressure or some other medical reason may have accounted for the fact that when I got out of the pool and dressed I was nearly busting with happiness. I walked back to the house, and when I stepped inside it was so quiet that I wondered if anything had gone wrong. It was not an ominous silence—it was just that I wondered why the clock should sound so loud. Then I went upstairs and found Marcie asleep in our bedroom. She was covered with a light wrap that had slipped from her shoulders and breasts. Then I heard Henry and Katie's voices, and I went to the back bedroom window. This looked out onto the garden, where a gravel path that needed weeding went up a little hill. Henry and Katie were there. Katie was scratching in the gravel with a stick—some message of love, I guess. Henry had one of those broad-winged planes—talismanic planes, really—made of balsa wood and propelled by a rubber band. He twisted the band by turning the propeller, and I could see his lips moving as he counted. Then, when the rubber was taut, he set his feet apart in the gravel, like a marksman—Katie watched none of this—and sent the plane up. The wings of the plane were pale in the early dark, and then I saw it climb out of the shade up to where the sun washed it with yellow light. With not much more force than a moth, it soared and circled and meandered and came slowly down again into the shade and crashed on the peony hedge. 'I got it up again!' I heard Henry shout. 'I got it up into the light.' Katie went on writing her message in the dirt. And then, like some trick in the movies, I saw myself as my son, standing in a like garden and sending up out of the dark a plane, an arrow, a tennis ball, a stone—anything—while my sister drew hearts in the gravel. The memory of how deep this impulse to reach into the light had been completely charmed me, and I watched the boy send the plane up again and again.

"Then, still feeling very springy and full of fun, I walked back toward the door, stopping to admire the curve of Marcie's breasts and deciding, in a blaze of charity, to let her sleep. I felt so good that I needed a drink—not to pick me up but to dampen my spirits—a libation, anyhow—and I poured some whiskey in a glass. Then I went into the kitchen to get

173

some ice, and I noticed that ants had got in somehow. This was surprising, because we never had much trouble with ants. Spiders, yes. Before the equinoctial hurricanes—even before the barometer had begun to fall—the house seemed to fill up with spiders, as if they sensed the trouble in the air. There would be spiders in the bathtubs and spiders in the living room and spiders in the kitchen, and, walking down the long upstairs hallway before a storm, you could sometimes feel the thread of a web break against your face. But we had had almost no trouble with ants. Now, on this autumn afternoon, thousands of ants broke out of the kitchen woodwork and threw a double line across the drainboard and into the sink, where there seemed to be something they wanted.

"I found some ant poison at the back of the broom-closet shelf, a little jar of brown stuff that I'd bought from Timmons in the village years ago. I put a generous helping of this into a saucer and put it on the drainboard. Then I took my drink and a piece of the Sunday paper out onto the terrace in front of the house. The house faced west, so I had more light than the children, and I felt so happy that even the news in the papers seemed cheerful. No kings had been assassinated in the rainy back streets of Marseille; no storms were brewing in the Balkans; no clerkly Englishman—the admiration of his landlady and his aunts—had dissolved the remains of a young lady in an acid bath; no jewels, even, had been stolen. And that sometime power of the Sunday paper to evoke an anxious, rain-wet world of fallen crowns and inevitable war seemed gone. Then the sun withdrew from my paper and from the chair where I sat, and I wished I had put on a sweater.

174

"It was late in the season—the salt of change was in the air—and this tickled me too. Last Sunday, or the Sunday before, the terrace would have been flooded with light. Then I thought about other places where I would like to be—Nantucket, with only a handful of people left and the sailing fleet depleted and the dunes casting, as they never do in the summer, a dark shadow over the bathing beach. And I thought about the Vineyard and the farina-colored bluffs and the purple autumn sea and that stillness in which you might hear, from way out in the Sound, the rasp of a block on a traveler as a sailboat there came about. I tasted my whiskey and gave my paper a shake, but the view of the golden light on the grass and the trees was more compelling than the news, and now mixed up with my memories of the sea islands was the whiteness of Marcie's thighs.

"Then I was seized by some intoxicating pride in the hour, by the joy and the naturalness of my relationship to the scene, and by the ease with which I could put my hands on what I needed. I thought again of Marcie sleeping and that I would have my way there soon—it would be a way of expressing this pride. And then, listening for the voices of my children and not hearing them, I decided to celebrate the hour as it passed. I put the paper down and ran up the stairs. Marcie was still sleeping and I stripped off my clothes and lay down beside her, waking her from what seemed to be a pleasant dream, for she smiled and drew me to her."

To get back to Marcie and her trouble: She put on her coat after the meeting was adjourned and said, "Good night. Good night . . . I'm expecting him home next week." She was not easily upset, but she suddenly felt that she had looked straight at stupidity and unfairness. Going down the stairs behind Mackham, she felt a powerful mixture of pity and sympathy for the stranger and some clear anger toward her old friend Mark Barrett. She wanted to apologize, and she stopped Mackham in the door and said that she had some cheerful memories of her own involving a public library.

As it happened, Mrs. Selfredge and Mayor Simmons were the last to leave the board room. The Mayor waited, with his hand on the light switch, for Mrs. Selfredge, who was putting on her white gloves. "I'm glad the library's over and done with," he said. "I have a few misgivings, but right now I'm against anything public, anything that would make this community attractive to a development." He spoke with feeling, and at the word "development" a ridge covered with identical houses rose in his mind. It seemed wrong to him that the houses he imagined should be identical and that they should be built of green wood and false stone. It seemed wrong to him that young couples should begin their lives in an atmosphere that lacked grace, and it seemed wrong to him that the rows of houses could not, for long, preserve their slender claim on propriety and would presently become unsightly tracts. "Of course, it isn't a question of keeping children from books," he repeated. "We all have libraries of our own. There isn't any problem. I suppose you were brought up in a house with a library?"

"Oh yes, yes," said Mrs. Selfredge. The Mayor had turned off the light, and the darkness covered and softened the lie she had told. Her father had been a Brooklyn patrolman, and there had not been a book in his house. He had been an amiable man—not very sweet-smelling—who talked to all the children on his beat. Slovenly and jolly, he had spent the years of his retirement drinking beer in the kitchen in his underwear, to the deep despair and shame of his only child.

The Mayor said good night to Mrs. Selfredge on the sidewalk, and standing there she overheard Marcie speaking to Mackham. "I'm terribly sorry about Mark, about what he said," Marcie said. "We've all had to put up with him at one time or another. But why don't you come back to my house for a drink? Perhaps we could get the library project moving again."

So it wasn't over and done with, Mrs. Selfredge thought indignantly. They wouldn't rest until Shady Hill was nothing but developments from one end to the other. The colorless, hard-pressed people of the Carsen Park project, with their flocks of children, and their monthly interest payments, and their picture windows, and their view of identical houses and treeless, muddy, unpaved streets seemed to threaten her most cherished concepts—her lawns, her pleasures, her property rights, even her self-esteem.

Mr. Selfredge, an intelligent and elegant old gentleman, was waiting up for his Little Princess and she told him her troubles. Mr. Selfredge had retired from the banking business —mercifully, for whenever he stepped out into the world today he was confronted with the deterioration of those qualities of responsibility and initiative that had made the world of his youth selective, vigorous, and healthy. He knew a great deal about Shady Hill—he even recognized Mackham's name. "The bank holds the mortgage on his house," he said. "I remember when he applied for it. He works for a textbook company in New York that has been accused by at least one Congressional committee of publishing subversive American histories. I wouldn't worry about him, my dear, but if it would put your mind at ease, I could easily write a letter to the paper."

"But the children were not as far away as I thought," Charlie wrote, aboard the *Augustus*. "They were still in the garden. And the significance of that hour for them, I guess, was that it was made for stealing food. I have to make up or imagine what took place with them. They may have been drawn into the house by a hunger as keen as mine. Coming into the hall and listening for sounds, they would hear nothing, and they would open the icebox slowly, so that the sound of the heavy latch wouldn't be heard. The icebox must have been disappointing, because Henry wandered over to the sink and began to eat the sodium arsenate. 'Candy,' he said, and Katie joined him, and they had a fight over the remaining poison. They must have stayed in the kitchen for quite a while, because they were still in the kitchen when Henry began to retch. 'Well, don't get it all *over* everything.' Katie said. 'Come on outside.' She was beginning to feel sick herself, and they went outside and hid under a syringa bush, which is where I found them when I dressed and came down.

"They told me what they had eaten, and I woke Marcie up and then ran downstairs again and called Doc Mullens. 'Jesus Christ!' he said. 'I'll be right over.' He asked me to read the label on the jar, but all it said was sodium arsenate; it didn't say the percentage. And when I told him I had bought it from Timmons, he told me to call and ask Timmons who the manufacturer was. The line was busy, and so, while Marcie was running back and forth between the two sick children, I jumped into the car and drove to the village. There was a lot of light in the sky, I remember, but it was nearly dark in the streets. Timmons' drugstore was the only place that was lighted, and it was the kind of place that seems to subsist on the crumbs from other tradesmen's tables. This late hour when all the other stores were shut was Timmons' finest. The crazy jumble of displays in his window—irons, ashtrays, Venus in a truss, ice bags, and perfumes—was continued into the store itself, which seemed like a pharmaceutical curiosity shop or fun house: a storeroom for cardboard beauties anointing themselves with sun oil; for cardboard mountain ranges in the alpine glow, advertising pine-scented soap; for bookshelves, and bins filled with card-table covers, and plastic water pistols. The drugstore was a little like a house, too, for Mrs. Timmons stood behind the soda fountain, a neat and anxious-looking woman, with photographs of her three sons (one dead) in uniform arranged against the mirror at her back, and when Timmons himself came to the counter, he was chewing on something and wiped the crumbs of a sandwich off his mouth with the back of his hand. I showed him the jar and said, 'The kids ate some of this about an hour ago. I called Doc Mullens, and he told me to come and see you. It doesn't say what the percentage of arsenate is, and he thought if you could remember where you got it, we could telephone the manufacturer and find out.'

" 'The children are poisoned?' Timmons asked.

" 'Yes!' I said.

" 'You didn't buy this merchandise from me,' he said.

179

"The clumsiness of his lie and the stillness in that crazy store made me feel hopeless. 'I *did* buy it from you, Mr. Timmons,' I said. 'There's no question about that. My children are deathly sick. I want you to tell me where you got the stuff.'

" 'You didn't buy this merchandise from me,' he said.

"I looked at Mrs. Timmons, but she was mopping the counter; she was deaf. 'God damn it to hell, Timmons!' I shouted, and I reached over the counter and got him by the shirt. 'You look up your records! You look up your God-damned records and tell me where this stuff came from.'

" 'We know what it is to lose a son,' Mrs. Timmons said at my back. There was nothing full to her voice; nothing but the monotonous, the gritty, music of grief and need. 'You don't have to tell us anything about that.'

" 'You didn't buy this merchandise from me,' Timmons said once more, and I wrenched his shirt until the buttons popped, and then I let him go. Mrs. Timmons went on mopping the counter. Timmons stood with his head so bent in shame that I couldn't see his eyes at all, and I went out of the store.

"When I got back, Doc Mullens was in the upstairs hall, and the worst was over. 'A little more or a little less and you might have lost them,' he said cheerfully. 'But I've used a stomach pump, and I think they'll be all right. Of course, it's a heavy poison, and Marcie will have to keep specimens for a week—it's apt to stay in the kidneys—but I think they'll be all right.' I thanked him and walked out to the car with him, and then I came back to the house and went upstairs to where the children had been put to bed in the same room for company and made some foolish talk with them. Then I heard

Marcie weeping in our bedroom, and I went there. 'It's all right, baby,' I said. 'It's all right now. They're all right.' But when I put my arm around her, her wailing and sobbing got louder, and I asked her what she wanted.

" 'I want a divorce,' she sobbed.

" 'What?'

" 'I want a divorce. I can't bear living like this any more. I can't bear it. Every time they have a head cold, every time they're late from school, whenever anything bad happens, I think it's retribution. I can't stand it.'

" 'Retribution for what?'

" 'While you were away, I made a mess of things.'

" 'What do you mean?'

" 'With somebody.'

" 'Who?'

" 'Noel Mackham. You don't know him. He lives in Maple Dell.'

"Then for a long time I didn't say anything—what could I say? And suddenly she turned on me in fury.

" 'Oh, I knew you'd be like this, I knew you'd be like this, I knew you'd blame me!' she said. 'But it wasn't my fault, it just wasn't my fault. I knew you'd blame me, I knew you'd blame me, I knew you'd be like this, and I . . .'

"I didn't hear much else of what she said, because I was packing a suitcase. And then I kissed the kids good-by, caught a train to the city, and boarded the *Augustus* next morning."

What happened to Marcie was this: The evening paper printed Selfredge's letter, the day after the Village Council meeting, and she read it. She called Mackham on the telephone. He said he was going to ask the editor to print an answer he had written, and that he would stop by her house at eight o'clock to show her the carbon copy. She had planned to eat dinner with her children, but just before she sat down, the bell rang, and Mark Barrett dropped in. "Hi, honey," he said. "Make me a drink?" She made him some Martinis, and he took off his hat and topcoat and got down to business. "I understand you had that meatball over here for a drink last night."

"Who told you, Mark? Who in the world told you?"

"Helen Selfredge. It's no secret. She doesn't want the library thing reopened."

"It's like being followed. I hate it."

"Don't let that bother you, sweetie." He held out his glass, and she filled it again. "I'm just here as a neighbor—a friend of Charlie's—and what's the use of having friends and neighbors if they can't give you advice? Mackham is a meatball, and Mackham is a wolf. With Charlie away, I feel kind of like an older brother—I want to keep an eye on you. I want you to promise me that you won't have that meatball in your house again."

"I can't, Mark. He's coming tonight."

"No, he isn't, sweetie. You're going to call him up and tell him not to come."

"He's human, Mark."

"Now, listen to me, sweetie. You listen to me. I'm about to tell you something. Of course he's human, but so is the garbage man and the cleaning woman. I'm about to tell you something very interesting. When I was in school, there was a meatball just like Mackham. Nobody liked him. Nobody spoke to him. Well, I was a high-spirited kid, Marcie, with plenty of friends, and I began to wonder about this meatball. I began to wonder if it wasn't my responsibility to befriend him and make him feel that he was a member of the group. Well, I spoke to him, and I wouldn't be surprised if I was the first person who did. I took a walk with him. I asked him up to my room. I did everything I could to make him feel accepted.

"It was a terrible mistake. First, he began going around the school telling everybody that he and I were going to do this and he and I were going to do that. Then he went to the Dean's office and had himself moved into my room without consulting me. Then his mother began to send me these lousy cookies, and his sister—I'd never laid eyes on her—began to write me love letters, and he got to be such a leech that I had to tell him to lay off. I spoke frankly to him; I told him the only reason I'd ever spoken to him was because I pitied him. This didn't make any difference. When you're stuck with a meatball, it doesn't matter what you tell them. He kept hanging around, waiting for me after classes, and after football practice he was always down in the locker room. It got so bad that we had to give him the works. We asked him up to Pete Fenton's room for a cup of cocoa, roughed him up, threw his clothes out the window, painted his rear end with iodine, and stuck his head in a pail of water until he damned near drowned."

Mark lighted a cigarette and finished his drink. "But what I mean to say is that if you get mixed up with a meatball you're bound to regret it. Your feelings may be kindly and generous in the beginning, but you'll do more harm than good before you're through. I want you to call up Mackham and tell him not to come. Tell him you're sick. I don't want him in your house."

"Mackham isn't coming here to visit me, Mark. He's coming here to tell me about the letter he wrote for the paper."

"I'm ordering you to call him up."

"I won't, Mark."

"You go to that telephone."

"Please, Mark. Don't shout at me."

"You go to that telephone."

"Please get out of my house, Mark."

"You're an intractable, weak-headed, God-damned fool!" he shouted. "That's the trouble with you!" Then he went.

She ate supper alone, and was not finished when Mackham came. It was raining, and he wore a heavy coat and a shabby hat—saved, she guessed, for storms. The hat made him look like an old man. He seemed heavy-spirited and tired, and he unwound a long yellow woolen scarf from around his neck. He had seen the editor. The editor would not print his answer. Marcie asked him if he would like a drink, and when he didn't reply, she asked him a second time. "Oh, no, thank you," he said heavily, and he looked into her eyes with a smile of such engulfing weariness that she thought he must be sick. Then he came up to her as if he were going to touch her, and she went into the library and sat on the sofa. Halfway across the room he saw that he had forgotten to take off his rubbers.

"Oh, I'm sorry," he said. "I'm afraid I've tracked mud—"

"It doesn't matter."

"It would matter if this were *my* house."

184

"It doesn't matter here."

He sat in a chair near the door and began to take off his rubbers, and it was the rubbers that did it. Watching him cross his knees and remove the rubber from one foot and then the other so filled Marcie with pity at this clumsy vision of humanity and its touching high purpose in the face of adversity that he must have seen by her pallor or her dilated eyes that she was helpless.

The sea and the decks are dark. Charlie can hear the voices from the bar at the end of the passageway, and he has told his story, but he does not stop writing. They are coming into warmer water and fog, and the foghorn begins to blow at intervals of a minute. He checks it against his watch. And suddenly he wonders what he is doing aboard the *Augustus* with a suitcase full of peanut butter. "Ants, poison, peanut butter, foghorns," he writes, "love, blood pressure, business trips, inscrutability. I know that I will go back." The foghorn blasts again, and in the held note he sees a vision of his family running toward him up some steps—crumbling stone, wild pinks, lizards, and their much-loved faces. "I will catch a plane in Genoa," he writes. "I will go back. I will see my children grow and take up their lives, and I will gentle Marcie—sweet Marcie, dear Marcie, Marcie my love. I will shelter her with the curve of my body from all the harms of the dark."

Set in Linotype Caledonia
Format by Anita Walker
Manufactured by The Haddon Craftsmen, Inc.
Published by HARPER & BROTHERS, *New York*